GW00456496

Driven to Death

A Finch & Fischer Mystery

J. New

Driven to Death
A Finch & Fischer Mystery Book 5

Copyright © J. New 2023

Cover design: Elizabeth Mackay
Interior Formatting: Jesse Gordon

ONE

The countryside was quiet and peaceful, with only the rhythmic swish of Penny's boots through the grass breaking the silence. A bright Saturday August morning with a light breeze was perfect for a brisk morning walk. There had been a shower of rain overnight and Fischer, her little white and tan Jack Russell Terrier, snuffled through the damp grass soaking his fur, but he was deliriously happy to be out walking through the fields and lanes. He stopped every so often and looked back, checking Penny was still following, then nose to the floor, he picked up another tantalising scent and set off in pursuit. His rear end waggling and his tail a blur.

With still a mile to go before she reached Thornehurst Grange, she heard the first distant chants of the protesters carrying on the air, rising and falling as they made their objections known. Fischer heard it too and stopped. Front leg held up and ears pricked at this strange noise. He gave a little whine and turned to look at Penny.

"Don't worry, Fish Face, we won't stay long. But I think, just to be safe, you'll have to go back on your lead for a while."

Fischer came trotting over and sat obediently while she clipped the lead to his harness, before they both marched on towards the noise.

Cresting the top of Sugar Hill, they caught the first sight of the demonstration on the country lane leading to the large Grade II listed building. The crowd was much bigger than the previous year. In fact, it was larger than any year Penny could remember, with the road lined on both sides by people waving placards. Starting from the gates of the Grange and backing up the road maybe a quarter of a mile. It was certainly much louder than it ever had been, Penny thought. She marched on, undeterred, with Fischer trotting happily by her side. Her intention was to add her support to the group of people opposed to The Glorious Twelfth. The start of the Grouse shooting season. She carefully made her way down the north slope of sugar hill and came onto the road leading to Pike's farm. Turning away from the direction of the farm, she strode alongside the grouse moor and turned into the road leading to Thornehurst Grange.

It wasn't long before she came upon the first of the protesters. They were spread out initially, but became more densely packed the closer she got to the gates of the estate. They were a mix of age groups, with a few faces she recognised from previous years, but the majority were strangers. Many were old hippie types in a sea of tie-dye, wearing baggy clothes and old festival tee shirts. Banners were held aloft in support of animal welfare and the end to barbaric blood sports. Some demanded peace and others had taken the opportunity to voice their political affiliations. Penny spotted an anti-vivisection banner displaying a mosaic of distressing images which turned her stomach. While she agreed completely with their stance, she was against having the pictures thrust in her face. It saddened her more when, as now, there were kids in the crowd. But then again, they no doubt saw it regularly at home.

Picking her way through the crowd, Penny eventually reached the imposing front gates of the Grange. The stone pillars on either side of the tall black iron barriers were old and solidly built, but looked to her as though they'd been pressure washed. The local yellow stone was not as dark or stained as when she'd last visited. The gate, too, was looking refreshed, the heavy metal work showing signs of having been recently sanded down and given a fresh coat of black paint.

The gate house on the right had also been spruced up. The stone cleaned and the frames of the tiny windows that faced the road shone with a high gloss finish in blinding white. Major Colton, resident and owner of Thornehurst Grange, had clearly made preparations for the start of the season. Keen to impress those who were prepared to pay exorbitant sums of money for the privilege of staying in the historic house and joining the first day's shoot.

Penny's feelings on the issue were clear. As an animal lover and vegetarian, she abhorred the violence of the annual grouse shoot. She'd expressed her views to the major in the past during one of their many friendly conversations. But a place like Thornehurst Grange was a money pit and needed huge sums for its annual upkeep. This was the way the major raised the finances. Penny felt there were better, non-violent ways to

J. New

achieve the fundraising targets, but the major wouldn't be budged.

So this was Penny's way of adding her support to the protest. She never raised her voice or waved a banner. Her presence and silent objection were enough. But she felt out of place this year. There was a current of underlying tension, a frisson of something she couldn't put a name to, but that could potentially turn violent at any moment. It worried her.

After half an hour, she decided it was time to leave. The crowd had almost doubled since she'd arrived, and she sensed more trouble in the air.

Penny pressed past a couple of young girls wearing black cropped puffer jackets and skirts that would be more use as belts.

"Excuse you," one of them snapped in a needlessly hostile tone.

"Don't mind me, just passing," Penny replied with a friendly smile.

She picked up the pace along the road away from the grange and as she reached the end where the crowds thinned out, she saw a pair of constables talking to a man in a suit. Penny recognised him, not only by the fact he was wearing a suit, which was his normal attire while on duty, but by his broad shoulders and neat hair. As though sensing her somehow he turned and Fischer let out a joyful little yap, straining on his lead to reach his friend.

Detective Inspector John Monroe greeted Penny with a warm smile and walked towards her, bending to give Fischer, who was trying to climb his trouser leg as usual, an ear scratch and a fuss.

"What are you doing here, Penny? Did you take a wrong turn coming down Sugar Hill?"

Penny smiled. "I always come here, same day every year. I need to show my opposition to this so-called sport. I can't, in good conscience, let it happen on my doorstep without expressing my objection."

John's smile slipped a little and Penny detected a brief hint of something that wasn't quite disappointment, but close flash across his face before he nodded and his honest, friendly smile returned.

"I'm just a little surprised to see you here, that's all. From a community point of view, I would have thought you'd be supportive of a big day like this?"

Penny raised an eyebrow. "Really? And just what is it about me you've learned in the last few months that would make you think I'd support cruelty of this kind?"

"It's a big local event and a huge bonus for the local economy. You're always so engaged with the local affairs. I just thought you would at least accept it. Welcome it even."

"But it's a blood sport, John. Frightening poor birds, then shooting them just for the satisfaction of some complete strangers with ideas above their station and the inability to find something more worthwhile to spend their money on. If this went on in the city, for example, it would be seen for what it is, a senseless massacre of sentient animals. It's cruelty. But set it in the countryside and everyone suddenly thinks it's some grand tradition and perfectly all right."

"But it is a grand tradition," John replied. "It's been the sport of kings for nearly two hundred years. It's the epitome of Britishness. It's good for the environment. If it wasn't for this annual shoot, this grouse moor wouldn't be preserved as it is."

Penny shook her head. She was disappointed to learn not only of John's views, but the fact he hadn't done the proper research.

"It's not natural, John. In fact, it's wholly unnatural. This should be upland meadow, flowers and grasses, teeming with life. But it's almost dead. There are only a few species of plant here, all preserved for one animal, the red grouse. This land is burned to keep out the vegetation they don't like. Predators are killed, foxes, stoats and weasels. Birds of prey, too. The red kites over at Cringle Wood are constantly in danger from the trapping that goes on here just to protect these poor birds. Purely so outsiders can come in and kill them."

John considered Penny's argument and nodded. Responding calmly. "All land is managed to a certain extent. There is still a lot of wilderness in the countryside. This is a small grouse moor, and it brings a huge boost to the area. A few days of shooting and Thornehurst Grange can finance its upkeep for another year. You must agree the old building is a thing of beauty and an important part of our heritage? It would be dreadful if it fell into disrepair and was lost because the major could no longer manage the bills. I hear the section of roof above the library has several leaks. There are a lot of important and irreplaceable old books there that could be damaged." Penny shook her head as John used the one argument he knew would hit home. She was the local mobile librarian and her love of books had no bounds. He continued. "This day's shoot alone will pay for the roof repairs. I think the preservation of the area's cultural history is worth putting up with a few city chaps coming down here to play at being the country gent for a week or two."

"Tell that to the birds," Penny said. "I don't object to people visiting the area, John. Quite the opposite. I am always happy to welcome visitors. What I object to is the blood sport. There are far better ways to raise the funds needed for the grange. I've given several worthwhile ideas to the major myself."

John smiled and nodded. "I do understand, Penny. Perhaps we can agree to disagree on this?"

"Yes, all right. It's obvious we're on opposite sides of the fence on this one, and I don't want to argue with you. Let's call a truce."

Penny looked away over the gathering and swelling horde. She noticed the puffer jacket and hip hop crowd, if that was the right terminology, and the hippies were not mixing. This was not one protest group. There were two distinct posses here, both consisted mainly of visitors to the area.

"You know, it's an odd mix of protesters this year," she said. "I'm familiar with travelling types, the hippies and the alternative lifestyle animal rights crowd, but these youngsters, in their urban fashions, look out of place. I wonder what they're here for?"

"They aren't here for the protest. They're fans of Max Damage."

"Who?"

John grinned. "It's not often I know something that's going on that you don't. Please, allow me to savour the moment. I don't know when I'll get another chance."

Penny thumped him playfully. "All right smarty-pants, spill the beans."

"Max Damage is a pop music star. Actually, I don't think pop music is the right phrase. Grunge or grime or something. He's coming for the shoot. This lot are the fans that have come to see him arrive. Which should be any time now."

"Max Damage?" Penny said to herself. She'd never heard of him. She wasn't really familiar with the music either, apart from knowing it was urban, combining rap and heavy beats. Something in the back of her mind said it was associated with violence in some way, although she might be wrong about that. Either way, it was definitely not her sort of thing.

Then she saw a black stretch limousine coming slowly up the road. The Max Damage fans swarmed around the car, whooping and punching the air. Banging on the windows and taking pictures with their phones. Though what sort of image they were likely to get through the blacked-out windows was anyone's guess.

Suddenly the sun roof slid back and the man himself stood up. The limo slowed down even further, creeping forward through the crowd. Max Damage lifted something above his head and roared. It was a customised golden shotgun, glinting sharply in the sunlight. The stock was encrusted with gold and sparkling gems. The crowd went wild.

"God, I hope that thing isn't loaded! Sorry, Penny, duty calls. I need to stop this before it gets out of hand."

John walked alongside the limo and called up to the musician, who was incessantly whooping and punching the air. There were also a couple of constables walking with him as the car proceeded at a leisurely pace through the centre of the crowd. Max Damage was pretending not to hear John's instruction, but even Penny could hear the DI's firm voice over the boisterous fans. His instructions were clear. John Monroe was insisting the young music star put away the shotgun or it would be confiscated.

As the car moved forward, the urban music fans and the animal rights protesters were jostling one another to get to the car, one group to admire the other to admonish. Penny lost sight of Monroe but heard him make one more appeal to Max Damage, and this time he did as he was asked, lowering the gun to the interior of the vehicle. But the young celebrity continued to whip up his fans into a dangerous frenzy.

Penny heard angry shouting and cussing as the two sides of the demonstration clashed. She caught a brief sight of John, one hand clutching his mobile phone to his ear, the other clamped over his free ear in an attempt to block out the surrounding cacophony.

A moment later, two police cars drove into the road from where they'd been parked out of site and eight police officers emerged and began to manage the crowd.

Penny was worried about John's safety and hated to leave, but there was nothing she could do. The officers needed to control the situation before it turned into a full blown riot.

She scooped up Fischer and held on tight. "Come on, little man, time to go."

Fischer looked back at the crowd and whined.

"He'll be fine, Fish Face. We don't want him to have to worry about us as well. Let's go home and put the kettle on."

More cars were arriving now containing the rest of the shooting guests. They slowed and came to a halt in a traffic jam caused by the protesters and fans near the main gate. Penny inched forward, but because of the crowds, she was forced to come to a standstill adjacent to a large, gas guzzling 4 x 4 off-road vehicle. The window was rolled down, and a man stuck out his head, waving a clenched fist. He was well into middle-age with wild red curly hair, receding slightly. He almost head butted Penny's shoulder. He made no apology, didn't give her a second glance, but looked up the road, shouting angrily.

"Get a move on!" His face was crimson with frustration and probably excessive living, Penny thought. Red veins on his cheeks and nose suggested an over-indulgence of alcohol that had gone on for many years. Her supposition was proved when he took a healthy swig from a silver flask. As Penny stood waiting to move on, clutching Fischer, who despite his dislike of crowds seemed quite happy in her arms, she heard another voice from inside the car.

"Get back inside, Sammy, and shut the window."

"Listen to me, little brother," the man called Sammy said. "It's the only way you can get through to these types of people. The local police are idiots. They won't know what to do unless we tell them." He leaned out again. "Move these bloody protesters now. Arrest them, for god's sake!"

"Sammy, for crying out loud, get in here. You're making a scene," the other man said, between clenched teeth.

Penny could see into the other side of the car. A man with the same wild, ginger hair but slimmer, neater and far more healthy looking.

"What?"

"Get in, now, or I won't listen to this latest business proposal you're so eager to share with me."

"There's no need for threats, Bobby. You won't listen to it, anyway. But it's a great idea. We'll both be rich."

"I am rich. As you were once, dear brother, in case you'd forgotten. But you squandered the lot. I don't know if I should invest my money in another one of your get rich quick schemes."

"Why not? You have enough to spare."

"I won't if I keep investing in your bad business ideas."

"See, you won't even discuss it properly. You've already made up your mind."

"You already have a hefty allowance. Mother and father would turn in their graves if I cut you off. It's for their sake I'm keeping you afloat. Come on, I've always looked after you, haven't I? You've got more than enough to keep you going without throwing everything away on the next madcap idea."

"I don't want handouts, Bobby, don't you get it? I want to make something of myself."

"Spending my money on foolish business schemes is not making something of yourself. Now, for crying out loud, shut that window and stop making a spectacle of yourself."

"Yes, Robert," Sammy said sarcastically, his lip curled.

The window began to rise as the crowd once again began to move. Penny would be glad when she was away from it all. Although she'd need to keep Fischer in his lead as the first shoot would be starting as soon as the paying guests were through the gates and settled. It wouldn't be too long, by the looks of things. Already the queue of traffic was beginning to move forward again.

Penny reached the end of Thornehurst Grange road and turned back on to the one leading to Pike's farm. She put Fischer down, much to his delight, and walked briskly on, happy to hear the clamouring of fans and protesters fade into the distance.

Eventually she came to a country footpath which she followed, taking her around the shoulder of Sugar Hill and alongside the moor. She climbed the hill that overlooked Pike's farm where the grouse were reared for the shoot and observed the moor itself.

The shooting would start soon, and she wanted to be as far away as possible by then. She'd had her morning walk, she'd registered her protest at the grange. Now she just wanted to be back at home in Cherrytree Downs, sitting in the garden with a good book and cup of tea. Fischer dozing at her side.

Her little companion let out a whine and looked up at her with chocolate brown eyes. This was where he was normally free to run around. What was going on?

"I know, Fischer. I'd love to let you off, but it's for your own safety. There's stupid people with guns, and I don't want them to spook you." She crouched down, taking his little head in her hands as she kissed his nose. "And I don't want you to get her hurt. Once we're at the other side of the hill, well away from the shooting, I'll let you go and you can run all the way home if you want. Okay?" Fischer licked her nose in response.

She laughed and stood up. South West she could see the roofs of Cherrytree Downs in the distance. The air was clear and bright with sunshine in a cloudless sky, the red rooftops of the old village standing out like bright confetti in the green landscape. From where she stood, she could trace the roads of the old village and find her little cottage. Using that landmark, she could easily find the roof of her parent's house and from there her friend Susie's. She could make out the shops surrounding the village green and caught the glint of sunlight on the duck pond. She spied the dark spot on the old stone tiled roof of the Pig and Whistle, the oldest building in the area with the proud designation of being the oldest pub in the country.

Penny glanced back at Thornehurst Grange and saw the first shooting party emerge from the ornamental gardens out onto the wild moor.

The grouse moor belonging to the grange was one of the smallest in the country. It was renowned for being exclusive and as such, only a small number of guests could use it at any one time. And due to its geography, a walking shoot was the preferred method, with the guests scaring up the birds themselves as opposed to a team of beaters advancing ahead.

Even from this distance Penny could make out music star Max Damage, his golden shotgun glinting in the sun. He was with two others, one tubby, the other slim. Penny concentrated, her hand shading her eyes, trying to make out the detail, then recognised the pair as the brothers who had been arguing over some sort of business deal in their off-road vehicle earlier. The slimmer one was wearing olive-green clothing, the perfect camouflage to sneak up on the unwitting birds. Long-sleeved tee-shirt, combat trousers and a multi-pocketed gilet. The tubby one had gone all out to look and play the part of a country squire, in tweed breeks, wellington boots, shooting gloves and a tweed shooting waistcoat over a brown checked shirt. Max Damage, on the other hand, had made no attempt at all to blend in. He wore a black tee-shirt emblazoned with his own face and name in white. Skin tight black jeans and a pair of black and white designer trainers.

Suddenly, she saw movement from the far side. From her vantage point, she could take in the whole vista. It wasn't possible to identify the person, but the clothing suggested it was one of the protesters. Dark and baggy. Unlike those that had travelled from outside the area, this person appeared to know the area well. They entered the moor through a perimeter hedge, a thick ancient farm land boundary. She watched as they pulled back an arm and launched something onto the moorland.

Penny wiped her face as a sudden breeze brought tears to her eyes. Then a moment later, she saw a thick plume of crimson smoke begin to build, drifting slowly on the wind towards the three advancing gunmen.

The smoke was growing thicker, a huge billowing cloud of red, rising slightly in the air but mainly flowing across the landscape. Suddenly, the moor was quickly lost from view beneath a carpet of smoke the colour of blood.

The cloud rolled on and soon Penny could just about see the three men waving their hands, trying to dissipate the smoke. But it was still growing thicker. She knew this was a protest tactic to disrupt the shoot, and while it would be abandoned to allow the smoke to clear, it wasn't a permanent solution. A safety hooter sounded from the building, a sign the shooting party needed to return to the grange immediately. It had never, in all the times Penny had been coming to the start of the season, ever sounded.

On the far side of the cloud, Penny saw the protester who'd created the smoke run into the cloud. While at the grange, the next line of shooters were waiting their turn. The breeze changed and suddenly she felt the smoke sting her eyes. She turned her head, rubbing her face, and in that instant heard a gunshot. A loud crack. Muffled by the distance and echoing off the hills and the side of the stately home. In between blasts of the hooter, she swore she heard shouting and someone calling for help.

Fischer tugged the lead towards the sound of the shot.

"No, Fischer," Penny said.

Another shot rang out. Echoes reverberating around the valley. Then the cloud was all around her. It had dissipated now to a fine mist, but it still stung her eyes. She covered her mouth, trying not to breathe it in. She had no idea what it was. As she tried to rub her eyes on the sleeve of her coat, Fischer's lead slipped from her grip and he went bounding off into the smoke, barking.

"Fischer, no! Come here!" He was still barking, not with excitement, but with urgency. Penny ran after him, deeper into the red haze.

As she moved deeper and lower down into the valley, the smoke grew thicker, making it hard to see more than a few yards. The hill behind was lost now. Away to her left, maybe half a mile, stood Thornehurst Grange. It, too, was entirely hidden from view.

Fischer continued to bark for her, and she moved forward in the direction of his increasingly frantic yapping. She was trying to go as fast as she could on the uneven ground, but one tumble or trip over a hillock could result in a broken ankle, and that was the last thing she needed.

A bird leapt into the air, startling her as much as she had startled it. She was obviously now right in the middle of the moor. This would be an incredibly dangerous place to be if not for the safety hooter sounding at intervals calling a temporary halt to the shoot.

Fischer barked again and Penny staggered forward, exhausted. It was a long time since she'd moved this fast over such a distance. Walking was fine, but she was not a runner. Especially over such difficult terrain, running through acrid smoke and with one arm over her face. But fear for her little dog had adrenaline coursing through her veins and had given her a heightened sense of awareness.

Abruptly, she saw Fischer through the smoke. He looked back at her, tongue lolling as he panted. In front of him lay the figure of a man.

Penny dashed forward, half afraid of what she would find. Fischer glanced back and forth between her and the prostrate figure. Undeniable concern etched his little face.

She looked down into the wide, frightened eyes of the slimmer, curly haired brother she'd heard in the car. He was fighting for breath, his mouth opening and closing. He moved in minute twitching movements, his eyes staring at her, entreating her for help. His shirt was red with blood, a large hole in his chest. She dragged off her jacket and pressed it to the wound, trying to staunch the flow of blood. With the other, she grabbed her phone.

"I'm calling an ambulance. Try to hang on. I'm with you. I've got you," she said soothingly, trying to keep the rising panic from her voice.

The man moved his mouth to speak and then was still. His sightless, vacant eyes turned upwards to the sky as the red smoke thinned and finally drifted away.

TWO

Penny closed her eyes and bowed her head. She knew full well the life of this man had slipped away before her very eyes. She pulled Fischer close, holding him on her lap. Taking comfort from his warmth and the beating of his little heart.

She'd had an awful feeling earlier at the demonstration that the day would result in some sort of violence. A broken nose or black eyes. Perhaps broken ribs as a result of fighting between the two factions. But never once did she think it would end in someone shot to death.

She heard voices calling out, drawing closer, and opened her eyes. Her glance rested on the hand of the dead man and she noticed the pale band of skin where a ring had once been worn.

The voices drew closer and the approaching footfall rustling through the coarse grass was a welcome distraction. The smoke still lingered, and she felt her eyes watering from the sting. She heard a man's heavy breathing, laboured after a dash across the moorland, then a voice called out. A voice she recognised and her heart lifted.

"John," she called out in reply. "I'm over here."

Fischer wriggled in her arms, whining, and she let him go. He bounded in the direction of the voice and returned a moment later with John Monroe and two constables following close behind. John crouched next to her and put his hands on her shoulders.

"My god, Penny, are you all right? Are you hurt?"

"No, I'm not hurt. I'm okay. I'm glad you're here."

"Come away," he said gently.

"The ambulance is on the way." Penny looked up. "But I'm afraid it's too late." She looked back at the man lying before her. "He's been shot in the chest, John."

Monroe took her hand and helped her to her feet. He gently guided her away from the body.

"I need to preserve the scene, Penny."

Penny nodded dumbly. "What an awful accident."

"Yes. Possibly. I won't know for sure until we've investigated."

"Fischer, come here little man," Penny called out. But Fischer had caught a scent a few yards away from the body and ignored her call. She walked over to him. "What is it, Fish Face?" Penny dropped to her knees where Fischer had been sniffing and saw a number of small metal balls camouflaged in the tufts. She picked up a few and found they were still warm to the touch. "Are these shot gun pellets?" she asked, turning to John, who'd walked over to see what the little terrier had found.

Monroe held out his hand, and Penny rolled the handful of metal balls into his waiting palm.

"Lead shot," Monroe said. He wrapped them in his handkerchief. "These could be important evidence. Well done, Fischer. We might have missed them if it wasn't for your exceptional nose."

Fischer looked up with bright eyes and gave a single woof. Then bounded further across the moor where he stopped, staring down at the grass, tail wagging, but the rest of him stock still.

"Now what has he found?" John said.

They both trotted over to the dog and found him guarding a shotgun.

John shook his head in bewilderment. "I don't know how he does it. We should have him on the force."

"I think you may have said that before," Penny replied.

"And I'm only half joking. I'm beginning to think he's part human."

Penny called Fischer away, giving him a huge fuss and a treat for being such a clever boy. Then clipped the lead to his harness. Monroe donned a pair of nitrile gloves and picked up the shotgun. He held it confidently and pointed away from those in the vicinity. He broke the barrel and made the weapon safe. A pair of spent cartridges jumped out, followed by a wisp of grey smoke. Monroe hooked the broken shotgun over his arm and stooped to retrieve them, slipping them into his jacket pocket. Penny watched as he did so. Surprised he seemed so at home around shotguns. Perhaps it was his police training? She knew she'd heard at least two shots, maybe three, but she couldn't be absolutely sure. Perhaps the last had been an echo? Were the shots fired from this gun?

She turned, looking toward the horizon as the smoke finally cleared and suddenly saw a figure running away. She was sure it was the same person who had thrown the smoke bomb. They disappeared over a rise in the landscape and were lost from view.

"John! Over there," she said, pointing. "Someone is running away."

John grabbed his phone and made a call.

"I'm on the grouse moor at Thornehurst Grange. We've got a runner leaving a crime scene. Get a car en route..." he hesitated, casting around, trying to get his bearings.

"That's Chiddingborne over there," Penny said, pointing. "About three miles away."

"On the Chiddingborne road from the moor. Suspect currently on foot, but may have a vehicle stashed nearby," he barked into the phone.

Penny turned and spied a mound of feathers, mottled brown and white, blending in with the coarse grass. She walked over.

"Careful where you step, Penny," John called out, who'd also seen the feathered bodies.

Penny nodded, looking down sadly at the grouse. Not one, but four birds lay in a neat little line. She frowned. How very odd.

"Penny."

She turned and walked back to John.

"I'll take you back to the grange once the ambulance has arrived. What were you doing out here?"

"I was on the hill trying to rub the smoke from my eyes when I let go of Fischer's lead. He ran off, and I followed him.

I got lost in the smoke and didn't even realise where I was until I scared a bird."

"And you just happened to find yourself next to the victim?"

"Not exactly," she replied, a little defensively. "Fischer found him and barked until I got there. He was alive when I arrived, but died soon after. There was nothing I could do."

"Sorry, Penny, I didn't mean to sound accusatory. From what I saw, you did everything you could." He squeezed her shoulder affectionately. "Try to take solace in the fact he at least wasn't alone."

A wailing siren in the distance announced the arrival of the ambulance, and they both turned to watch as two paramedics made their way over the moor. John met them at the body and, after a short conversation, they loaded the stretcher and covered the remains with a sheet. The left hand fell loose for a moment and once again Penny saw that faint band of white where a ring had been until fairly recently.

"Come on, let's get you back," John said, putting an arm around her shoulder and guiding her back towards the house.

"So you weren't out here with the intentions of disrupting the shoot?"

Penny shot him an indignant look, about to give him a mouthful, when she saw the twitch of his lips.

"Very funny. I might not agree with it, but I'm not in the habit of sabotage. This was dangerous. Three men with loaded guns, blind in a fog of thick smoke, is asking for trouble. Look what just happened. I did hear a cry for help after the first bang."

"The first bang?" John asked in surprise. "There was more than one? How many did you hear?"

"I'm positive I heard one. Then I heard shouts for help. Then a second bang. The safety hooter was going off at the point, so I knew I'd be all right on the moor. I mean, someone needed help, John. I couldn't just ignore it. Besides, I had to find Fischer. There may have been another bang, but with the wind, the smoke, the hooter and the echoes, I'm not entirely positive."

"I think it's pretty unlikely you heard shouts from a man with a shot gun wound to his chest. Even if it didn't kill him outright like you said, he wouldn't have had the strength to shout. He would have been having enough trouble simply breathing."

"I'm sure I heard shouting, John. Sound carries well over these moors in the summer. It must have been before the hooter started."

John nodded, but Penny could tell he wasn't completely convinced. She was beginning to doubt herself now. But if she did hear calling, and it wasn't the victim, then who on earth had it been?

Back at the grange, the guests were all gathered on the wide stone-flagged terrace overlooking the ornamental gardens and the moor beyond. Several newly painted white wrought-iron tables had been laden with elevenses. With self-service pots of tea and coffee.

Two police constables were talking to the men who had

been in the victim's group. It was the man's brother, Sammy, the chubby red-haired man Penny had overheard in the car and the music star Max Damage.

As the constables confiscated the shotguns, putting them in evidence bags, Max Damage took umbrage.

"Hey, be careful with that. It's worth more than a year of your wages, your house and car combined. Real gold and diamonds that is. I want it back without a scratch, you hear? Anyway, I don't know what you want it for. I was back here at the house as soon as the smoke started. Never even fired the damn thing. Can't risk breathing that stuff in and ruining my voice. So I wasn't even on the moor when the shooting started. Everyone saw me." Max pointed to one of the other guests, an elderly gentleman wearing Tweed Breeks and a matching jacket. His ear defenders were still looped around his neck even though he'd not had a chance to use them. "You saw me, didn't you, mate?"

The elderly man turned away with a frown on his face as though he hadn't heard helped himself to coffee.

Sammy was rubbing his eyes. They were red and puffy from tears, probably a combination of the irritating smoke and grief from the loss of his brother. Penny felt a pang of sympathy for him.

"I need to go and flush this stuff from my eyes," he said, pressing one of his hands to his face, covering eye and cheek.

The constable looked to Monroe for approval, and he nodded. She was new and quite young, but Penny could see the determination in her face to do a good job.

"So, tell me what you saw, Mr Damage?" Monroe said.

"I never saw anything," he said in a city drawl that Penny

felt was more affectation than genuine. He sucked his teeth after every sentence as though they were full stops. "I heard the safety hooter not long after the smoke started and was already on my way back. I don't know what happened out there."

When Sammy returned, Monroe immediately asked about the cut under his eye. The man had washed his face, but a small, nasty gash was clear and a bruise was already starting to develop.

"I think I tripped when I was walking back through the smoke."

Monroe frowned.

"You think?"

"No, I did. I'm sure I did. I was confused, what with the smoke and the hooter. The grass isn't like a lawn, you know. It's rough stuff and grows uneven. But never mind my eye. What are you doing to catch my brother's killer? I saw them run off into the smoke. Have you caught them yet?"

Monroe nodded, making notes.

"We're investigating every lead and sighting. We'll get them, Mr Reynolds, you can be sure of that. I will ask for a formal statement shortly, but in the meantime, are you planning on leaving the county?"

Sammy shook his head.

"No. We booked in here for the week and I'm staying until this murderer is caught."

Monroe turned to Max, who shrugged.

"I'm here all week, too. Shooting, fishing and working on some new material. A bunch of new tracks that'll drop this winter."

Monroe scribbled.

Max sucked his teeth.

Monroe moved away, followed by Penny and Fischer, and was immediately approached by Major Colton.

"Dreadful business, Detective Inspective," he said, nodding to Penny. "Simply dreadful. I can't believe it."

"Did you know Mr Robert Reynolds well, Major?" Monroe asked.

"Oh yes, I think so. He was a regular guest here at Thornehurst. A big supporter over many years. He'll be missed, Monroe. It's a bad do. Very bad." Major Colton shook his head, scuffing the flagstone with the toe of his boot. He looked up. "So, when do you think we can continue with shoot? Obviously the guests have paid good money to be here and I don't want to leave 'em waiting any longer than I have to, if you get my drift."

Penny almost shook her head. What the Major didn't want was people asking for refunds. No doubt the money had already been spent.

"The scene is isolated for now, Major," Monroe replied. "We'll need to carry out a fingertip search of the area, but I will release the moor back to you as soon as possible. I'm aware of how important it is to you and I'll endeavour not to have matters go on for longer than necessary."

"Righto, old chap. I'll let them know," the major said with a smart salute to John and a nod to Penny before he wandered back to mingle with his guests.

"So you're treating it as murder, John?" Penny asked.

Monroe nodded.

"Oh yes. There's no doubt in my mind that someone deliberately shot and killed Robert Reynolds. The question now is who?"

THREE

Penny slept uneasily all night, plagued by images of dead men chasing her through blinding red fog while her dog called frantically to her from far ahead. Her feet pumping, she never seemed to move forward, as though she were running on a treadmill. She woke drenched and tangled in the sheets. The window was open, and the voiles were gently swaying in the early morning breeze.

The book she had been reading slipped off the bed as she moved and landed on the floor with a thump. The sound of gunshots echoed in her mind. How many had there been? One, Two, more?

She turned to look at the clock. It wasn't quite 6 am. The sun would be rising over the rooftops of the village shortly. In a couple of hours, the bell ringers at Winstoke would start calling the congregation to morning service.

She yawned and rubbed sleep from her eyes. They felt better this morning. As soon as she'd got home the day before, she'd showered and rinsed the last remains of the smoke from her face and eyes. She'd checked Fischer over, but oddly he hadn't seemed affected at all. She'd taken a damp flannel to his eyes, though, just in case. He hadn't particularly liked it, but had sat patiently while she wiped his face, knowing he'd get an extra special treat afterwards.

She felt a thump, thump, thump on the bedclothes and looked round. Fischer was laid down, but looking at her with bright button eyes, his tail banging furiously.

"Good morning, happy little man," she said.

Fischer jumped up and bounded over to lick her face. Penny giggled, trying to push him away.

"Yes, all right, I'm up. Breakfast will be ready in two shakes of a Fish Tail!"

She slipped out of bed and grabbed her summer dressing gown, slid her feet into the flip-flops that acted as slippers during the summer, and went downstairs. Fischer raced on ahead, claws tapping on the floor as he danced in front of his food cupboard.

"I think you should go and do your business outside first," Penny said, opening the back door.

Fischer sped out and was back within seconds, waiting by his bowl. Penny burst out laughing.

"Don't tell me you did anything in that short amount of time. That was pretend, wasn't it? Crikey, Fischer, I think John's right. You are part human. Okay, you can have breakfast first."

After a leisurely breakfast of tea and toast for Penny and a speedy, didn't touch the sides, one for Fischer, Penny went upstairs to get dressed while her little dog pottered about in the back garden.

Half an hour later, she was ready.

"Let's go and see mum and dad, shall we?"

Fischer sped off and was back a moment later with his lead in his mouth. Penny ruffled his head.

"Good boy."

It was only half past seven and few people were up and about in the village. A young girl with the morning papers stopped to say hello to Fischer, the bag of Sunday papers with their supplements almost as big as she was.

Her parents were already up and about by the time she arrived. Her mother pulling open the door before she was even half way down the garden path.

"I don't know how you do it, mum. You always open the door before I even knock."

"I was coming down the stairs, and I saw you on the path," Sheila Finch said.

She crouched down, taking Fischer's head in her hands, and gave him a cuddle.

"Come on in, love. Do you want some tea? Have you had your breakfast yet?"

Inside, her dad was at the dining table, a copy of the weekend edition of The Winstoke Gazette open in front of him.

"Morning, love. Morning, Fischer," he tapped the paper with his finger. "Susie has written a piece on the shooting at Thornehurst Grange yesterday. Have you read it?"

Penny kissed the top of her dad's head and sat at the table next to him.

"Already? She must have been up all night getting that written for today's issue. No, I haven't read it yet. I can't keep up with her work. She seems to write the entire paper herself these days. What with the children and her job, I don't know how she finds any time for herself."

Her mother entered with a tray of tea.

"Terrible news at the grouse shoot," she said, putting the tray in front of Penny and hovering over her husband's shoulder, reading the article. "Did you know about it, Penny?"

Penny paused and both her parents shot her a quizzical look.

"Actually I was there. Fischer and I found the victim."

"Oh, not again," Sheila said.

"You?" her father said. "At the grouse shoot?"

"I wasn't shooting the grouse, dad," she replied, rolling her eyes.

"You weren't at the protest again, were you?" her mother said. "From what I've heard, it was complete bedlam."

"I was there at the protest. I go there every year as you well know. I can't sit by and let it go on without making my feelings known. But yes, it was chaos. Much worse than previous years."

"Some things are worth shouting about, if you believe in it that strongly."

"I wasn't shouting. Mine was a silent protest. In fact, I left as soon as it began to get out of hand. Anyway, I was on the north side of Sugar Hill overlooking the moor when I heard a call for help. I found the man with Fischer's help. But there was nothing I could do."

"Oh, how awful, Penny. Are you all right?"

Penny nodded.

"I'm fine, mum, don't worry." She didn't let on she'd

watched him die. Her parents worried enough about her as it was.

"You should leave this sort of thing to the police. It sounds dangerous."

Her father reached out and laid a gentle hand over Penny's.

"We still worry about you, love. Even though you're all grown up and left the nest years ago, you're still our daughter."

"I know, dad. I wouldn't put myself in danger deliberately."

Her father looked at her and raised an eyebrow. His expression said he didn't believe her for a minute. And if past experiences were anything to go by, he was right not to, thought Penny. She'd got herself in no end of trouble snooping into other cases.

"I've never been on a protest in my life," he said. "But I am proud of you for sticking up for what you believe in."

Her mother returned with another tray.

"Susie's article doesn't say how the accident happened."

"It wasn't an accident," Penny said. "John Monroe was there. He told me he thinks it was murder."

Sheila disappeared and came back a moment later with another huge tray. This one was full of toast, a butter dish, and several types of marmalade and fruit preserves.

"Right, dig in, Penny."

Penny looked at the tray. There was enough toast here to feed the whole village.

"Mum, you've not done all this just for me, have you?" she said, not disclosing the fact she'd already had toast once that morning. It always tasted better at her mum and dad's anyway, for some reason.

"Don't be silly. It's for all of us."

"You know, I remember the Reynolds brothers," Albert said, reaching for the strawberry jam. "Always together in town years ago. When they were younger. Well, we were all a lot younger then. You were just a girl, Penny. Samuel always appeared to be loitering outside the pub on market street. Liquid lunches that seemed to go on for most of the day. But his brother Robert was a different story. Very focused on business. He had a little office above a pet shop on market street with a side entrance on Druid Lane. After I'd had a late night working at the shop, I'd come back that way and his light was always on. I'd see him pacing back and forth. Never spent a penny on anything that wasn't necessary. That's what sticks in my mind."

"I don't remember them at all," Penny said.

"You were still in school," Sheila said. "It was before you'd even taken your exams when the Reynolds brothers moved away."

"That's right," Albert said. "Robert Reynolds' business outgrew Winstoke pretty quickly."

"What did he do, dad?"

"Financial investment of one sort or another. Helping local businesses invest and grow initially. I know a lot who used him, most of them successfully, but it wasn't something I wanted to get involved in. At the time, it sounded a little too good to be true. It worked for his brother Sammy, though. He made a small fortune in one big deal. I'm not sure how much of it he managed to keep hold of, though. He wasn't one for hard work, wasn't Sammy, the polar opposite of Robert, and he certainly liked to spend it. Not in a generous way, either. He spent it all on himself. Flash cars, the latest big expensive toy."

Sheila tapped her husband's arm.

"That's right, I remember now. He landed a remote control plane in the village duck pond one year. An accident as far as it went. He lost control of it from up on Sugar Hill. PC Bolton was new at the time and he made a huge fuss about it."

"And rightly so, love. The ducks had chicks for one thing, and that plane was the size of my first car. It wasn't a toy. If that had come down in the high street and hit someone, they'd have been seriously injured, or worse. It was an irresponsible thing to do. What a waste of money."

"What happened? Was in confiscated?" Penny asked.

"This is PC Bolton we're talking about, Penny," her mum said. "He might have been new to the job, but he still had an aversion to proper work, and confiscating that plane, or fining Sam Reynolds would have meant paperwork. So no, nothing was done. Sammy came and collected it and went on his merry way with a flea in his ear from Bolton, but nothing more serious than that."

"These two sound so different. It's hard to believe they are brothers at all." Penny said, smearing another slice of toast with lemon and lime marmalade.

Albert nodded. "I always thought the same, love. Robert poured all his money into the business and, as soon as it was big enough, moved the whole shebang to the big city. Although I believe he came back on occasion to visit his friends and fellow business owners from the old days. He was a very wealthy investment banker at the end. All that money." Her father shook his head sadly. "Money is important, but it can't buy happiness. Neither of them ever married. Bachelors to their core. I'm not sure either brother was truly ever happy in their lives."

FOUR

Monday morning and Penny and Fischer were up with the larks. Her mobile library was headed to Rowan Downs first thing, and she had a fresh stock of books she knew her regulars would be eager to get their hands on.

She jumped in the driver's seat. Fischer happily sitting on the passenger side and turned the key. The engine spluttered and failed to start. Fischer gave her a worried look. She tried again, pumping the gas pedal a couple of times, being careful not to flood the engine, and this time it burst into life.

"Well, that's a bit worrying, Fish face. I think the old book mobile needs a service. I'd better get it checked over by my friendly mechanic soon.

She reached Rowan Downs bang on time and no sooner had she opened the side doors than she was greeted by the arrival of the two eminent ladies of the village, Mrs Lillian Greaves and Mrs Harriet Ward. It was barely nine o'clock and already they were bickering about something or other.

"I tell you, Harriet, those Reynolds boys were both bad," Lillian Greaves said, bustling forward.

"Nonsense. Not the younger one, Lillian. He wasn't bad. He was a very hard worker," Harriet retorted, taking a step in front of her friend to reach the library first.

"What good is it to care for work more than you care for people?" Lillian asked, quickening her pace to get a fraction ahead.

Penny smiled broadly, highly amused at the antics of the two old women.

"Good morning, Ladies," she said, insinuating herself between them so they didn't push one another into the road and break a limb.

"Good morning, Penny," Harriet said.

"And a good morning from me too, dear." Lillian added not to be outdone.

Penny helped them both into the library together so she wasn't accused of favouritism, which would no doubt result in yet another argument between the two friends.

"Oh, I think you have a wobbly shelf here, Penny," Harriet said.

"Always looking for fault," Lillian tutted, before adding, "and another loose one here, dear."

The ladies were right. It looked as though her library van needed maintenance everywhere.

"Where's that little dog of yours?" Lillian said. "We have a treat for him."

She glanced back at Fischer, who was lying on the front seat with his paws over his nose.

"Fischer," she called out, and a little head popped above

the back of the seat, before he jumped over to receive the gift the women had kindly brought him. It was wrapped in a blue and white striped bag, which Penny recognised immediately as the type the butcher used. Her stomach clenched a bit, but Fischer was a dog and a meat eater.

"Look what Mrs Greaves and Mrs Ward have brought you, Fish Face. A bone."

"Is it all right, Penny?"

"Of course it is, thank you so much. What do you say, Fischer?"

Fischer barked twice, spun in a circle, sat down and lifted his paw.

"Oh, he is a dear."

Fischer took his bone outside and disappeared under the van with it.

"Now, what books are you recommending today, Penny?" both ladies asked.

"I have something special for you this week."

The two ladies on their last visit had been waxing lyrical about a television program they loved, a historical crime series set in Victorian era London. Penny hadn't heard of it, but on her last visit to the main library in Winstoke, she'd discovered it was based on a series of books. She'd brought two copies of the first one for them to try. She handed them over.

"Oh, Penny, this is absolutely perfect, don't you think, Harriet?"

"I do indeed, Lillian. Penny, you have surpassed yourself. Thank you very much, my dear. We always know we can rely on you to bring us books we want to read."

"You're both very welcome," Penny said. "And if you like

the first, the good news is there are another six in the series to read. With more to come."

"How wonderful," the ladies said in unison.

"The very best thing about finishing a book you've thoroughly enjoyed is finding out it's part of a series," Harriet said.

"I couldn't agree more," Lillian said.

After she'd checked out their books and helped them back onto terra firma, Penny went to check the loose shelving. They really did need fixing. Not only were they a bit tired looking, they were dangerous. The last thing she needed was for them to fall on a customer. There was no funding available in the library budget, but she was sure she could fix them herself. And if not, she knew she could ask her dad. As Penny was trying to tighten the shelving to make it last a bit longer, another customer arrived. It was her old friend and teacher, Mr. Kelly.

"Hello, Penny," he said, stepping up into the van. "Having a bit of trouble, are you?" He nodded to the shelves.

"Unfortunately, I am. The shelves are loose. I'm just trying to get them tightened up as a temporary solution. The whole van needs some maintenance. She's an old bus and certainly gets a lot of use. It's only to be expected. So, what can I do for you today, Mr Kelly? Is there anything in particular you're looking for?"

"Nothing in particular. I'll just have a look and see what takes my fancy. I suppose you've heard what happened at the grange yesterday?"

"I was there, Mr Kelly. It's dreadful."

George Kelly nodded. "Hugh is beside himself. He called me last night in a state of shock and worrying about how it will impact the future of the shoot. It's the biggest fundraiser of the year for him." Penny remembered that Major Colton was related by marriage to Mr Kelly. The Major's wife, Christine, had been Mr Kelly's cousin. "The rumour going round is that one of the protesters murdered the victim," Mr Kelly continued. "Beggar's belief, doesn't it? You go to protest about the killing of animals only to go and shoot dead a person."

At the time, Penny had felt it likely the person she'd seen fleeing the scene had been one of the protesters, but listening to Mr Kelly now, she wondered if that was actually the case.

"Has anyone been arrested, do you know?" she asked, taking Mr Kelly's library card to check out the book he'd chosen.

"Not that I've heard. But here's someone who is sure to know." He nodded toward an approaching car. It was John Monroe. "Thank you for the book, Penny. I'll see you next week, if not before. If you decide to do a bit of sleuthing and need a partner, you know where I am."

She saw John park his car, then amble over with a smile on his face. She was ridiculously pleased to see him. Fischer shot out from his spot underneath the van just long enough to greet one of his favourite people, then dashed back to his bone.

"Morning, Penny."

"Hello, John. How are things?"

"Inching forward at a snail's pace at the moment. It's always the same at the beginning of an investigation. I wish it were otherwise, but it's a working visit, I'm afraid. I'm here to get your statement if you have time?"

"Yes, of course. It's quiet at the moment. Would you like a cup of tea? We could sit outside," Penny said, indicating the small camp table and chairs she'd positioned in the shade. "That way, I can see if any customers arrive."

"Tea would be great, thanks."

A few moments later, with a freshly brewed pot, Penny asked if there was any more news?

"I'll have the forensics back on the shotgun you found in a few days, along with the type of weapon used in the murder. Obviously, we can't categorically say the gun you found is the same one that killed Robert Reynolds at the moment. If it isn't, then it makes things even more confusing, so let us hope we can link the two. Can you start from the beginning, from when you got to the demonstration? Unless there's anything you noticed prior to that?"

Penny shook her head. "I didn't see anything on my walk over. Although I wasn't looking for anything out of the ordinary."

She poured them both tea, then started from when she joined Pike's lane, turning into the road leading to the grange and being surprised at the unusually large crowd of protesters there were this time compared to previous years. As she talked, John's fountain pen flew across the page in neat cursive. She then disclosed the conversation she'd heard between the brothers as she was leaving.

"So they had a disagreement about a business proposal?" John asked.

"I don't think it was a proposal as such. More an off the

wall idea Sammy had that he was asking his brother to invest in. I got the feeling it was yet another get rich quick scheme he had that Robert had no intention of funding. He'd lost money on previous ideas from what I could gather. You know they were local once upon a time? Not born around here, but former residents when they were both younger."

"So I gather. Winstoke wasn't it? Do you remember them?"

"No, I was still at school when they left. Mum and dad mentioned them on Sunday. They were chalk and cheese, by all accounts. Robert was heavily invested in work and reluctant to spend on anything except the business. And Sammy spending money like water on anything he could think of. Sammy also had a drink problem at that time. Judging from his complexion and general health, I'd say he still does."

"I noticed the same thing yesterday. I expect Major Colton is currently locking up his best brandy and hiding the key to the wine cellar." He turned over the page. "What happened next?"

Penny continued with her statement, eventually getting to the part where she found Robert Reynolds shot.

"Did he say anything, Penny?" John asked gently.

"Nothing. He was just staring, utter panic in his eyes. He knew he was dying. It was horrible. But I did hear someone call for help, John. In hindsight it probably wasn't Robert, but someone definitely did."

"I'm not doubting you. But we've found no one it could have been. I'm sorry."

"It's all right, John. Just as long as you don't think I'm going mad. What about the person we saw running across the moor? Did you find them? Was it one of the protesters?"

Monroe paused. "As much as I'd like to, I can't really mention any precise details at the moment. But we're looking for another person to help us with our inquiries."

Penny rolled her eyes and smiled.

"Very enigmatic."

John laughed.

"It's part of the job. Much like a politician. You say as much as you can without actually saying anything at all."

"And not answering direct questions," Penny said. "Is there a special school for that?"

"Oh, yes. It's quite an in-depth training course we have to go on."

There wasn't much more Penny could tell him after that. He'd arrived soon after and knew what had happened from then onwards.

"Listen," he said, putting away the signed statement. "It's going to be all hands on deck for now, but when things have calmed down a bit, would you like to go out dinner?"

He stood up, and Penny did the same. Feeling a rush of excitement.

"I'd love to. Just let me know when's best for you. Will you manage to make the quiz night on Thursday?"

"I shall do my absolute best."

He stepped forward, looked briefly around the village to make sure they weren't being watched, then drew her in and gave her a gentle kiss.

"I've been wanting to do that since I found you on the moor yesterday."

He gave her another quick kiss, then pulled away.

"Sorry, work calls. I'll see you soon. Look after yourself, Miss Finch."

Penny grinned.

"Likewise, Detective Inspector Monroe."

She watched him walk back to his car. He turned, gave her a quick wave, then drove away. Penny shook her self and called for Fischer. He crawled out from beneath the van, tail wagging.

"It's lunchtime. Let's go for a walk, Fish Face. I seem to have some pent up energy I need to get rid of."

Fischer bounded into the van and came back, dragging his lead. She clipped it on and gave him a pat, and after locking the van and grabbing her lunch box set out in the direction of Sugar Hill.

Penny ate a pasta salad as she walked, while Fischer bounded on ahead, but always checking Penny wasn't too far behind. After fifteen minutes she could see the gardens of Thornehurst Grange, the neatly manicured lawns and tidy flower beds. It looked so peaceful, idyllic. No one would have guessed it was the scene of a recent crime. She gazed over the moor, every detail of the previous day etched into her mind.

What did she actually know so far? The victim was a former resident of the area, although not born locally. He moved away with his brother many years ago but returned annually for the start of the grouse season at the grange. Only three people had walked out onto the moor for the first shoot. The Victim himself, his brother and the music celebrity. They each had a shotgun. They were quite far away from the building when it happened. Too far for anyone else to have shot Robert Reynolds. Unless someone had lain in wait?

There was the figure Penny had seen running across the moor, disappearing into the thick red smoke. The same person who'd thrown the smoke bomb? John still didn't know who it had been, but Penny was convinced they moved like someone with local knowledge. They were sure footed across the moor and seemed to know exactly where they were going. Penny felt almost positive they were looking for a local resident.

And how many shots had she actually heard? She stopped, thinking hard. Two definitely. Then there were shouts for help. Then she was pretty certain there had been a third shot deep in the red smoke, and no more cries of help after that.

And four dead grouse.

And one dead man.

FIVE

The three-mile drive to Chiddingborne after lunch was a leisurely one. With the passenger side window opened just enough for Fischer to stick his head out, he had a whale of a time with the breeze in his face and his ears flapping. His nose constantly twitching as it picked up tantalising smells from the surrounding countryside.

Penny pulled into her usual spot outside the post office and jumped out of the van. She immediately jumped back in again when a sudden squall brought with it a shower of chilly rain. She hurriedly wound up the windows and she and Fischer watched in amazement as the miniature weather system tore up the main village street like a tornado.

A minute later, the whirlwind had gone.

"Good grief, Fischer, I have never seen anything like that in my life. What on earth is happening to the world's weather? It must be global warming."

The little dog let out a woof of agreement. Unfortunately, the drizzle remained.

"I would never believe it was August," Penny muttered to herself. She climbed out of the van and opened the side doors just enough to show she was there and open, but not enough to ruin the books. She settled inside on a camping chair and reached for a book. It was just enough rain to put people off walking to the library, at least until the shower passed.

A regular customer did arrive though, braving the weather. And after shaking out her umbrella, stepped up into the van. Brenda always knew exactly what she was looking for and was quick to choose a complete series of well-known fantasy novels. The camper van wobbled on its suspension as she stomped back to Penny, her library card in hand.

"Hi Brenda."

"Afternoon, Penny. As you can see, I'm spending my summer holidays in Earthsea this year."

Penny handed her card back. "Have you read these before?"

"I certainly have," Brenda replied. "More than once, actually. The first time was many years ago when I was a kid on holiday. I haven't read them for a long time though and wanted to experience them again. If you've not read them, Penny, then take my advice and do so as soon as possible. They really are wonderful."

"I might just do that, Brenda, thanks."

Brenda flashed her a smile, packed her books in a 'keep calm and read on' bag, then stomped off into the rain that was getting heavier by the minute. It was time to shut the doors. Penny grabbed the sandwich board that announced the library was open, then closed the doors tight and resumed her reading to the accompanying sounds of the pitter patter of raindrops on the roof and Fischer's gentle snores from the front seat.

Then a drop of water landed on the page she was reading. She looked up. Another drip was hanging, ready to fall. The seam in the roof panels had a line of water running from the side above the door. Water was getting in somewhere and clinging to the ceiling in gravity defying rivers until at a rivet in the roof the water built up, and then...

Drip.

Another splash of water.

"Oh, no!"

Penny retrieved a packet of tissues from the glove compartment and wiped away the stream. It stayed dry for a moment before the water began to build up again. She searched the entire roof inside for a hole but failed to find where the water was getting in.

She had a tube of sealant at home that she'd used to plug a leak under her kitchen sink. For now, she'd just have to keep on top of it, mopping away the incoming water and protecting the books until she could get home and make some emergency repairs.

Fischer was now standing up with his paws on the back of the seat. He cocked his head as another drip of water hit the floor.

"Don't worry, little man, we won't be swimming anytime soon." Apart from the rain, Fischer didn't like water. Especially where it shouldn't be, like inside the normally warm, cozy and dry van. It stemmed from a nasty experience he'd had as a puppy. Before she'd rescued him. "We'll patch her up later when we get home." He still wasn't convinced and began to bark at the roof. She reached into a bag tucked under the driver's seat and got him a treat. He settled back down, chewing happily.

Penny continued to mop up and check for any water damage and by the time she'd scoured every square inch, the rain had stopped. Clouds parted over Sugar Hill and bright sunshine once again shone on the village.

Penny reopened the doors. The smell of fresh rain on the ground and the scent of flowers from the hanging baskets and potted plants outside the post office was beautiful. She stepped down and looked into the blue sky emerging from behind the clouds. The rain was moving off and she could see cloud bursts away to the west, dropping a fresh shower of rain over Winstoke. A rainbow emerged, bright and clear, one of the strongest she'd seen for a long time. Like something from a painting. With the sun so low in the sky Penny realised the day had worn on. She checked the clock on the dashboard and realised it was time to head home.

Just as she was closing up, she spotted Claire dashing out of her shop, the Treasure Chest, a few doors down from the post office. She had a book in her hand and was waving it frantically.

"Oh, I nearly missed you," she said. "At least I've saved the fine. Sorry I'm late, I had a job enlarging a ring for a customer and lost track of time. He's just left with it."

"Don't worry, I lost track of time as well today, otherwise I'd have popped in and saved you a job. Was the customer pleased?" Penny asked, taking the book.

"He was. It was a really beautiful piece. I was completely absorbed in it. A heavy gold band with an intricate Celtic knot of interwoven strands of gold on the top. It must have been a commission, because I've never seen anything like it. The gold would be worth its weight, of course, but it's impossible to put a price on a piece like that. It was such a pleasure." She suddenly slammed her forehead with her palm, her eyes widening. "Oh, I forgot about the cleaning. I wiped it before I started, but I'd planned to give it a proper clean and buff once I'd finished. I don't suppose you saw where he went, did you, Penny? It was only a moment ago."

Penny shook her head. "I'm sorry, Claire, I didn't. The roof of the van sprung a leak and I've been dealing with that."

Claire sighed. "He didn't leave any contact details and paid in cash. I don't have a name, address or number for him. And I haven't seen him around here before, either. He's definitely not from Chiddingborne. Oh, well. There's nothing I can do about it now. He was pleased with it, so that's the main thing. Hopefully, he'll come back. At least I remembered to return the book. Are you all done for the day now, Penny?"

Penny patted the side of the van. "A bit of maintenance to do when I get back, then a quiet Monday night in. What about you?"

"The same. Part two of that detective series is on tonight. So I'm putting my feet up and indulging. Goodnight, Penny, see you next week."

"Did you want a book before you go, Claire?"

"I'm all right today, thanks. I'll get one next week, though."

"Okay. Goodnight, Claire."

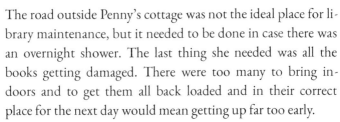

The road outside Penny's cottage was not the ideal place for library maintenance, but it needed to be done in case there was an overnight shower. The last thing she needed was all the books getting damaged. There were too many to bring indoors and to get them all back loaded and in their correct place for the next day would mean getting up far too early.

Once she was parked, she dashed up to the back garden shed and retrieved the small stepladder and the tube of sealant.

Back at the van, she immediately started hunting for the source of the leak. Or leaks, as the case may be.

Fischer sat at the side of the camper, happily watching Penny crawl about on the roof. She looked for a split or a crack, a hole. The paint was starting to flake in some areas, a few spots of rust were appearing on the edge of the roof. She sighed. The more she looked, the more she saw all the little defects and points on the van that needed some work. This would take more than a tube of sealant. She found a couple of patches of corrosion where the paint had completely worn away and the metal had rusted, bubbling up and making a small hole. It looked as though these two were the culprits. She smeared a small amount of sealant over the areas, making sure they looked as neat as possible.

"Maybe dad can lend us a hand," Penny said to Fischer as she clambered back down the ladder.

Fischer dashed inside the camper van and jumped back out, his lead in his mouth. Penny realised by mentioning her dad, she'd got her little dog's hopes up. She was too tired and hungry to visit her parents now. Besides, they were probably settled in for the evening. Not that they wouldn't enjoy a visit from them. But Penny just wanted to eat her dinner and relax.

She leaned down and gave him a hug, scratching his ears. "Sorry, Fish Face, not today. Come on, we'll go and get some dinner. Are you hungry?"

Fischer dropped the lead and barked loudly while dancing on all four paws. Penny laughed.

"I'll take that as a yes."

In bed later that night, with her little dog snoring on her feet and a book lying open in her hands, Penny thought about her van. She was worried. While her salary kept her going, there was little in the way of extra funds available in the library budget to extend to major repairs. She could continue to patch things up, but how long would they last? And the fact it had trouble starting that morning when it had never done that before was also nagging at her mind. The mobile library was an essential service to the residents of the outlying villages, particularly the elderly, who couldn't travel far. Its loss would be monumental. Not to mention Penny might very well be out of a job. She sighed and, marking her page, turned out the light. There was nothing she could do about it now. The best thing was to try to get some sleep and see what tomorrow would bring.

SIX

Things were always less troubling in the light of day and when Penny opened the curtains the following morning and was greeted with a bright sunny day, all fears of the leaking roof evaporated.

Tuesday was the day the library was due in Hambleton Chase, where she would spend the whole day. No need to re-locate for the afternoon. She would have her lunch in the village and looked forward to greeting her library regulars.

Reversing out of her parking space, she spotted a patch of oil on the road. Her heart sank, and she leaned forward in the driving seat and stared at the dark patch with a growing sense of dread.

"That wasn't there yesterday."

Penny doubled checked the dials on the dashboard. Both the oil and temperature gauges looked fine. She pulled the lever to release the engine hood and got out to investigate.

The dipstick showed minimal loss, but she topped it up just in case. Her dad would know what to do.

Penny felt her attention drift as she drove over to Hambleton Chase. Concern for her van was taking precedence over everything. She shook her head. One lapse in concentration and she could end up with more than a dripping roof and a leaky oil pipe to deal with.

Her early morning shift went as expected, with her regulars all turning up at their usual times. They were creatures of habit, and Penny could almost set her clock by them. Mid morning, a familiar yet infrequent visitor arrived. Cheryl Tait pulled up next to the library and got out of her car. Straight blond hair, limp and greasy, her lips thin and pale. She stepped inside and folded her arms. Defiant and aggressive from the outset. Penny took a deep breath.

Fischer stepped forward to greet the newcomer, but Cheryl took a step back and peered at him in disgust. He made himself scarce. He knew when he wasn't wanted.

"I need a cookbook," she said to Penny, glowering unnecessarily.

"Hello, Cheryl," Penny replied as sweetly as she could manage. "What are you cooking?" She perused her recipe book selection. It was small, but she was able to cover a surprising amount of culinary ground with a half shelf of carefully curated books.

"Grouse," she replied tersely. "I have guests who want to have the local birds from the shoot at Thornehurst Grange for dinner."

Penny felt her smile slip a bit. Of course, a local business like Thatchings, the guest house in Hambleton Chase, would want to show off the locally sourced food. On the bottom shelf she found a classic cook book, almost as old as Mrs Beaton's, that specialised in game recipes.

"I think you'll find something in there," she said, handing over the book. "If you follow the recipe, I'm sure your guests will be suitably impressed."

Cheryl scoffed and laughed without humor. "I'm not cooking them. I've enough to do without sweating over a hot stove. Cooking is Gary's job."

Penny had been at school with Gary Tait. He'd always been a sweet and shy boy. Now he was a hen-pecked and equally undemonstrative man. Penny couldn't help but feel sorry for him to have ended up with a wife as bitter and brash as Cheryl.

"Well, I'm sure he'll do a great job."

"Ha! I doubt that very much," she said, turning her back and leaving the van without so much as a goodbye.

"You can come out now, Fish Face. The witch has gone."

Fischer crawled out from beneath the van, tail wagging, and Penny gave him a treat.

The air was warm and the sky a perfect light turquoise with scudding clouds, causing shadows to race along the ground. Penny sipped a cup of tea while leaning against the van. She was miles away when Henrietta Shattock popped her head around the corner.

Fischer trotted over, tail wagging, and Penny gave her a double take. Her hair was in dreadlocks, finely woven with brightly coloured threads. She had a small silver ring in her nose and her clothes were what only could be described as colourful rags. They were like scraps, but on closer inspection Penny noticed they'd been beautifully hand stitched together to create a unique ensemble. Her heavy red ankle boots were old and battered, threaded with rainbow laces, and hand painted with flowers and butterflies. Penny could tell that for all the bravado and the 'look at me' wardrobe, beneath was a shy and nervous girl.

"Henrietta, it's been a long time since I've seen you at the library. How are you?"

"I prefer Henri now, actually," she said, confident but respectful.

Penny nodded. She understood. She preferred Penny to Penelope, her given name. Henri bent down and stroked and fussed over Fischer until he was practically demented with ecstasy. As soon as the girl stopped, he'd push his head into her hand asking for more.

"What brings you all the way out here, Henri?" Penny asked. "The main library is practically on your doorstep, isn't it? You still live in town with your father?"

Henri nodded. She was avoiding looking at Penny, focused entirely on the little dog who was lapping up the attention.

"Did you want a book?" Penny asked and noticed the way Henri shifted slightly. She was uncomfortable. "Or was there something else? You can have a look at what books I've got if you want."

She stepped into the van, followed by a reluctant Henri.

"It's mostly novels, but there are a few reference and non-fiction if that's something you're interested in."

"These shelves are a bit decrepit," Henri said, shaking one vigorously.

Penny held her breath, waiting for it to collapse completely. Luckily, it held, but only just.

"Yes, they need a bit of renovation."

"More than a bit. They're about to disintegrate." She looked up at the ceiling and pointed to the yellow stain. "And you've got water coming in." Henri looked around further. "This old thing is falling apart. Pity, she's a really nice vintage bus. A classic." For the first time, she looked directly at Penny. "I can fix her up if you like? I'm good at fixing things. I was better than all the boys at school in wood and metal work. Art too." Her eyes dropped.

"I don't doubt it. I can tell you're creative and good at making things. But that's not really why you're here, is it? You didn't know my van was in need of repair when you came."

"Are you investigating the murder?" She gave a shelf an exploratory wiggle.

"I'm not supposed to be investigating anything. The police don't want amateurs messing things up. Although I do want to know what happened as much as anyone else does."

Henri stepped down from the van, giving Fischer a final ear scratch.

"Is there anything you want to ask or tell me, Henri?" Penny said. "Do you know something about what happened at the shoot?"

Henri moved away.

"Tell me if you want me to fix your van. I keep my dad's running, no problem. I just want to make things better."

"I know you do," Penny said gently. She sensed Henri was holding back, but didn't want to push her. She was so skittish it would only take one wrong word from Penny for the girl to disappear and never return.

"I have to go," Henri said and walked away.

"Okay. Well, it was nice to see you again, Henri. You know where I am if you need a book or help with anything."

Henri waved over her shoulder before jumping into a small battered van with the name of her father's hardware store printed on the side. Shattock's of Winstoke.

"Well, that was odd, Fischer. Very odd. I wonder what she really wanted? I think she knows something but is either too shy or too afraid to share it. If I'm right, I think we'll be seeing young Henri again very soon."

SEVEN

Penny used the time in between customers to check the van and make a list of repairs along with what products and tools she'd need to fix them. Eventually the day was done, and she settled into the driver's seat, Fischer at her side.

At the other side of Rowan Downs she took a right onto the Winstoke road rather than drive straight on to Cherrytree Downs, and Fischer knew instantly this wasn't how Tuesdays normally went. He gave a small whine and looked at her, head cocked to one side.

"You are a clever little thing, aren't you? We're going to the hardware store in Winstoke to pick up some things to fix the poor van. It's in Knight's Lane, just off the market square, so not far."

Fischer seemed to settle down once she'd told him the plan, and she shook her head in amazement. He was definitely way above average intelligence for a dog. In fact, he was brighter than a few people she knew as well.

Town had a strange mid-week feeling about it. She normally came to the main library on a Thursday, her last working day, to stock up for the following week and with the weekend just around the corner, it always had a relaxed air. Today the mood was focused work energy.

She pulled into a parking spot at the end of Knight's Lane. It was a historic cobbled street featuring preserved medieval buildings, some dating as far back as the fourteenth century. The street was narrow, with many timer-framed buildings with jettied floors that overhung the street by several feet. Many of which were grade II listed. It was too narrow and old to allow parking, so a short walk lay ahead. She clipped Fischer to his lead, and they jumped down.

The old bell rang above the door when she pushed it open. The door was set in a timber frame and was the original from when it was built many hundreds of years ago. The bay window was the same, but both had been given a new coat of shining black paint since Penny had been in last.

The shop had a very distinctive smell. Oil and metal, glue and strangely, sawdust, which was odd as there didn't seem to be any about, not unpleasant, and the wooden floor had been polished and worn by generations of locals looking for that essential nut, bolt or screw to mend a much loved or much used object. This was an independently owned, quintessential DIY store predating any of the large chains that blighted the edges of so many towns nowadays.

At the sound of the bell, Mr Shattock appeared through a beaded curtain hung over a doorway behind the counter. He was in his early sixties, having become a father in his forties, but he looked at least a decade younger.

"Miss Finch," he said in greeting. "Nice to see you. How's that kettle holding up?"

Penny had bought her stove top kettle years ago from Shattock's and while she no longer used it, having upgraded to a funky new one which lit up with a pink LED light as the water boiled, it still worked as good new.

"It's a real gem, Mr Shattock. Works the same as it did when I first bought it."

"Good to hear. Now, what can I get for you today?"

"The mobile library is in sore need of attention. I've got a couple of leaks in the roof and various wobbly shelves."

As Penny spoke, Mr Shattock looked along the neat rows of shelving. He selected various tubes and put them on the counter. Pulled open drawers filled with brass screws, chose a few and then did the same for silver coloured ones. He laid them next to the tubes. And grabbed a few more items, adding them to the pile.

He explained what she would need to do to find, prepare, and seal the leaks. How to prepare and fill any chips in the wooden shelving and asked what sort of screws she'd prefer?

"Brass or galvanised steel?"

"I'm not sure, to be honest. Whatever works best and lasts the longest, I suppose."

Penny was beginning to realise how much the work would involve if it was to be done properly, and while she was reasonably good at DIY and would try her hand at most things, repairing the van which was her business really needed to be done by someone with more knowledge than she had. It would also take her far longer to do the work and she needed the van up and working quickly. Preferably without taking it off the road at all.

"You know, Mr Shattock, I think it would be better if I got someone else to do it. I don't want to make it worse. I saw Henri earlier, and she said she'd do it for me. I don't suppose she's here, is she?"

"She's out on a delivery at the moment, taking fertiliser and some other items over to Pike's farm. It's a big order this time. They must have made a fair bit of profit supplying Thornehurst Grange this year. Then she's fixing the gate over at the Manor House in your village. But I'm sure she'd be more than happy to do the work when she's free. She always liked you, Penny. She used to talk about you often after her mother... Well, my Henrietta has the mind of a scientist, an engineer and an architect combined. She can fix or make just about anything. She's only seventeen but has the skills of a master craftsman, or crafts person, should I say. I keep getting told I shouldn't be using such old-fashioned terms nowadays. She's just like her mother was: strong, independent and deter-mined. She told me she'd be driving by the time she was seventeen and she is. If she puts her mind to it, she can achieve anything."

"I always knew she was clever. She'd pop into the library and pick up really obscure titles on inventions. She was really interested in Joseph Bazalgette a few years ago, I seem to recall."

"Oh, yes, I remember. Not to brag, Penny, but my girl is a genius. I mean, just look at this." He pointed to a shelf in pride of place behind him.

Penny looked at the contraption housed in a brass case set with glass walls. Steel balls were rolling smoothly down a series of wooden chutes. Numbers were marked along the sides and a bell rang as one of the chutes tipped up on a pivot. Mr Shattock checked his watch.

"Right on time, as always. Henrietta built that. It's a kinetic chronometer. More commonly known as a rolling ball clock. She's already drawn out the plans for something similar using coins."

"That's absolutely amazing," Penny said in awe. "I couldn't even begin to fathom how she worked that out."

"It's all maths. I don't understand it either, but it's like second nature to Henrietta."

Penny looked at the selection of items on the counter.

"Would you mind if I speak to Henri before I buy anything? She'll know better than me what's needed."

"Not at all. That's probably for the best. I'll tell her you were here and have a job for her."

"Thank you, Mr Shattock."

Penny backed away from the counter and bumped into a small display table. She turned to steady whatever she'd knocked, but was too late. The table was past its tipping point. She reached out but wasn't fast enough. A wicker basket fell to the floor and a thousand grey balls scattered across the boards.

Fischer backed away, startled.

"Oh, Mr Shattock, I am so sorry. Let me clean it up for you."

Penny got on her hands and knees and started scooping up the mess. This was going to take hours. Mr Shattock went to retrieve a broom and, on his return, helped her to her feet.

"Don't worry about it, Penny. I'll have them all swept up in a jiffy.

Penny looked at the ball in her hand. It was nearly the size of a garden pea but a dull grey colour. She'd seen something similar recently.

"Is this the shot from a shotgun, Mr Shattock?"

"Ah, easy mistake to make, but no, they're lead balls. I keep a stock for the local fly fishermen, I mean fisher people," he sighed. "Anglers. They use them to make their fishing flies. Adds a bit of weight to them as they cast the fly over the water. But we've decided to stop selling them. They'll be recycled. Henrietta has convinced me lead is not good for the river."

"It looks a lot like shotgun pellet."

"It wouldn't make good shot. It's too soft. See here," he took the ball from Penny and indicated with the nail of his little finger. "It has a split in it so it can be fixed to feathers and a hook for the fishing. It wouldn't travel very far. I imagine you've heard about the murder at the grouse shoot?"

Penny nodded. "I was there when it happened, actually."

"I was sorry to hear Robert Reynolds had been killed. I don't bear a grudge, you know. Life's too short for that nonsense."

"Did you have a falling out with him?"

Mr Shattock leaned on his broom, settling in for a long story, Penny thought.

"Reynolds sold me a bad investment. I doubt you'll remember, but my wife and I used to run a small holding raising free range turkeys for Christmas. I lost the business after Reynolds convinced me to invest in a scheme of his. It was my own fault. Deep down, I knew it was a mistake, but I wanted a bit more security for my family. It seemed like a good idea at the time. Other businesses were getting good advice from Reynolds and making a bob or two and I didn't want to be left out, I suppose. I should have known not everyone can win in these kind of deals. But there you are. We get a little wiser with every year, a little wiser with every mistake." He looked around his small store. "I'm happy with this place. It's popular and we provide a good service locally. I wished I could have passed the turkey business onto my daughter though. But then again, I doubt she'd want it. She's a vegan and an animal rights activist. Nothing illegal, of course, but she joins the protests when she can. She's a clever little thing, but there's an edge of anger in her ever since her mother died. She'll calm down eventually, I expect."

"She's a teenager, Mr Shattock. It's perfectly normal. She's in the process of discovering who she is. She's a really lovely girl and obviously bright. I wished I had half her skill."

"Well, I'll let her know you want to speak with her. Look after that kettle."

"I will. Thank you. See you again."

Penny left with Fischer trotting alongside. Some elusive thought tickling the back of her mind.

EIGHT

After another dream filled night, Penny awoke early the next morning with a feeling of dread, wondering what the weather had been like overnight and what sort of state the van and its contents were in. Flinging open the curtains, she was relieved to see the sunshine and a cloudless sky. But more importantly, everywhere was dry. Not a drop of rain had fallen while she had been asleep.

Standing at the van, however, she was left in no doubt the oil leak, unlike the weather, had not improved. In fact, it was getting worse. She topped up the oil, then made a decision to go and see Martin at the garage in the village. She couldn't put it off any longer. The van needed a proper service and professional repairs.

She left Fischer at home while she ambled across the village and at the former police house, she found John Monroe standing outside. As though some sixth sense had told him she was there, he turned and waved.

"Good morning, Penny," he said, holding her close and giving her a quick kiss. "How are you feeling after what happened the other day?"

She clung to him briefly, enjoying the feeling for a moment of being held close, then pulled away.

"I'm fine, John, don't worry."

"I should have come to see you before now. I'm sorry. The case is taking up just about all my time at the moment."

"As it should be. You need to catch whoever killed Robert Reynolds. So, how is the investigation going?"

John smiled. "I can't keep anything from you, can I? Well, all right. I know you'll keep it to yourself. I received the first forensic report back last night. The shot Fischer found on the moor is lead. The shooters all used a cartridge the major had made specially a few years ago, which is steel shot. It's much better for the environment. So that means the lead balls Fischer found must have come from an older shoot."

"Really?" asked Penny, confused. "But they were found in a clump together. Surely they would have been scattered and buried in the soil if it was that long ago?"

Monroe nodded. "I agree, but either way, it wasn't the shot issued to the shooters that day."

"Another mystery then." She turned to the house. "Have you finished moving in?"

"Sort of. Most of my belongings are in there, but in boxes. I've not had a chance to unpack yet now I've a murder to solve. I only dashed over here quickly to let the movers in."

"Who are your suspects, if you don't mind me asking?"

"Obviously the two who were in Robert's group. His brother Sammy and Max Damage. But we're also looking for the person who set off the smoke bomb. We haven't managed to trace them yet. If you hear anything, will you let me know?"

"Of course."

Monroe's phone rang and, before he could make an excuse, Penny raised her hand and smiled.

"I know. Work. I'll see you later."

Monroe nodded a farewell and answered the call.

By the time Penny arrived at the garage, the huge double doors were open and Martin was buried in the engine of an old car.

"Good morning, Martin."

Martin looked up and grinned. Grabbing an old rag, he wiped the oil off his hands and wandered over.

"Now then, Penny. What can I do for you?"

"The van has an oil leak, and it's had a bit of trouble starting recently. Can you take a look?"

"No problem. It's probably time she had a full service anyway, if my memory serves me right?" Penny nodded. "Bring her in at the weekend and I'll take a look. I know you need it on the road for work during the week."

"Thanks, Martin, I appreciate it."

"No problem. My Gran would have my guts for garters if she knew the library was off the road when I could have fixed it."

Penny grinned. Martin's Grandma was one of her regulars and had a penchant for slightly raunchy romance novels. She left Martin to his work and headed off to start her day. It was Holt's End that morning. She was just setting out her camp table and chair when she saw Max Damage get out of his car and walk her way. He was squinting and walking a little uncertainly.

She bent down to straighten the chair leg and just as she stood up, the music star bumped straight into her.

"What the hell?" he said crossly. "Watch where you're going."

Penny bit her tongue. "I'm sorry. I thought you'd seen me."

Max glared, looking very slightly over her left shoulder. "What's that supposed to mean?"

Penny realised then that Max's eyesight was appalling. He confirmed it a moment later when he took a pair of glasses with thick lenses out of his pocket and put them on.

"I'm looking for the fishing lodge. The one by the lake. Where is it?"

His rudeness took her breath away, and she had to make a real effort to remain calm and polite. He obviously didn't recognise her.

"You're nearly there. You just took one turning too far. If you go back up to the main road and turn in the direction you came in, the entrance is a few hundred yards or so on the left."

"Right. And be careful who you're bumping in to next time."

He removed his glasses and gingerly made his way back to his black sports vehicle. Settled inside, he looked around my-opically, checking for onlookers, then once again put on his glasses. He drove off, gunning the engine and spinning the wheels. Utterly disturbing the peace and quiet of the village. She glanced under the van and found Fischer laying quietly but observing the proceedings.

A few seconds later, another car roared into the village. A black sports car and at first glance she was sure it was Max

Damage driving, but as the car slowed slightly to take a bend, she noticed the driver wasn't wearing glasses. He did look remarkably like the music star, though, although she realised now it wasn't. As the car sped away, yet another vehicle came roaring into the village, a small red hatchback filled with youngsters in black puffer jackets. They raced by, one hanging out of the passenger side window with his phone out, filming the black car racing away.

Penny stood in shock for a moment, waiting for more fans chasing the celebrity to ruin the peaceful morning, but thankfully no one else appeared to be in pursuit.

"I hope we don't get any more of that," she said to Fischer, who had crawled from beneath the van and was now under the camp table next to Penny's feet. "It's dangerous. Someone could get hurt."

After a quiet morning dealing with her regulars and a couple of new patrons, Penny and Fischer jumped into the van and left Holts End to go to Thistle Grange, her stop for the afternoon, and her lunch date with Susie.

It was always a welcome treat meeting her friend at the Pot and Kettle. She was seated in the bay window when she and Fischer arrived. After they'd ordered lunch and a bowl of water for Fischer, they caught up with one another's news.

"I bumped into Max Damage this morning," Penny said. "Literally."

"He's cruising around the area playing the country gent,"

Susie said, rolling her eyes. "What is it about these city types who like to play act at country living? I just don't get it."

"He was on his way to the fishing lodge when I saw him."

Susie had her reporter's notebook out and was scribbling down information as Penny spoke. "My editor has asked me to keep up with him, but his fans are all over the place trying to catch a glimpse or a photo they can upload to social media and he's put plans in place to thwart them. Do you know he's got four cars in the area and he's jumping from one to another in order to lose them? And he's got a driver who looks just like him. A doppelgänger. That's why we've had conflicting reports putting him in two places at once."

"Well, someone needs to stop it all, Susie. We've got a lot of elderly residents in these villages. Just imagine if one of them was crossing the road with their wheeled walker, or a wheelie shopping trolley, and a car came careening round the corner. They wouldn't be able to stop in time. It's dangerous. They have absolutely no respect for the villages or the countryside. I hope you'll put this angle in your article as well, Susie?"

"Of course I will. I always try to write a balanced report. You're right, they are a public menace. But, by the same token, having a celebrity in our midst is bringing in a lot of people who are spending in the local shops and establishments. It's a double-edged sword."

"I understand that, but they need to abide by the law. If I'm honest, at the risk of sounding like I'm an old fuddy-duddy, I'd never heard of him before the weekend."

Susie barked out a laugh. "Using the term fuddy-duddy isn't doing you any favours in that regard, you know. Actually,

I have heard of him, but only recently. It's not my sort of music. We didn't grow up on this stuff, Penny. I suppose that's the difference. Do you know what his real name is?"

"No idea."

"Maximilian Theodore Cavendish III. How's that for a mouthful?"

Penny laughed. "Almost as absurd as Max Damage. So, what have you discovered about him?"

"I had a chance to say hello earlier in the week. He was just coming onto Market Street from Knight's Lane. He wasn't happy about being stopped. A bit rude, actually."

"That's where Shattock's hardware shop is," Penny said.

Susie gave her a queer look and grabbed her arm.

"Oh no! You don't think he's into... DIY, do you?" The way Susie said it made it sound like the worst sin imaginable.

Penny gave her a playful push, grinning.

"No. But maybe he wants to make his own fishing flies." Then she wondered how he would manage if his eyesight was so poor?

"I doubt it. He'd be more likely to pay someone to do it for him. He's a rich kid from a wealthy family. A posh boy acting like a street thug to give the impression he's one of the lads and understands the struggles of today's youth. It's all fake."

"But what has he got to be so angry about?"

"Well, I do have news there. He could be losing the rights to his music. I've discovered Max Damage's failing London studio was bought out by Reynold's investment company. It appears the music and song rights could have accidentally been part of the deal." She leaned down and pulled a folder from her bag. "Then there's this. These are rare. But I know someone who can retrieve hard to find photos from the net. Max Damage has taken down as many as he could, but there are always traces and my guy came up trumps."

Susie laid the printed images on the table. They were early candid shots of the music star when he was still just Maximilian Cavendish. He was walking into an exclusive London dining club wearing a dinner jacket and bow tie. He had on a pair of thick lens glasses.

"According to a gossip column I unearthed recently, the rumour is he had laser eye surgery, but it went wrong. Now he's stuck with wearing these heavy glasses," Susie said.

"They don't quite go with his new persona, do they? And I understand why he'd be furious about losing the rights to his own music. But I still think he should act like an adult and not like a spoiled child."

"Fuddy-duddy," Susie said, grinning.

After lunch, Penny waved goodbye to Susie, who hopped in her car and gave Penny a friendly toot on the horn before driving back to the newspaper offices in Winstoke.

Stepping out from Cobbler's Lane, she ran into Mr Sheridan, and Fischer pulled on his lead and danced about excitedly to see his canine friends, Daisy and Gatsby, Mr Sheridan's young Labradors.

"Hello, Mr Sheridan. Nice to see you. I'm not running late, am I?"

"Hello, Penny. Don't worry, you're on time as usual. Would you believe I'm actually early for once?"

They walked back to the library together and just as Mr Sheridan was about to let the dogs off for a run around with Fischer, as they usually did on their weekly library visits, Penny stopped him.

"Maybe it's best not to let them off today. Unfortunately, the van has an oil leak, and I'd hate the dogs to get covered."

"Good thinking. I wouldn't like that either. Bathing these two makes a mess you wouldn't believe."

Fischer looked at Penny, curious as to why they were being denied their usual frolic around and under the van. But then he settled down outside and the two labs settled down with him.

"They accepted that with ease, didn't they?" Penny said. "Perhaps they know there's a problem this week?"

"Beneath their soppy and goofy exterior is a very clever animal. They're easy to train and fast learners."

"That's why they make such good guide dogs, I expect," said Penny.

"And gun dogs too. They were originally bred to retrieve birds, hence the name retriever. Mainly ducks, I'm led to believe, the purists prefer a pointer or setter for the grouse. But there are quite a few switching to Labradors now. They're very good at it."

Penny listened and smiled politely while her customer chose the book he wanted this week. A History of Hantchester County, with a chapter dedicated to the castle.

"I'm interested in learning more about the castle. It's been there my whole life, yet I know so little about it."

As Mr Sheridan departed, with his dogs trotting happily by his side, Penny sat in her camp chair with Fischer on her knee. Talking of guide dogs had made her think about Max Damage. She couldn't remember him wearing his glasses when he was waving to the crowds from the sunroof of his car. From the way he had acted when he'd asked for directions to the lodge, he was obviously embarrassed about them. But she also didn't remember him having them on while he was out shooting on the moor.

"Now why would he be trying to shoot grouse when he can't see more than five feet in front of his face?" she asked Fischer. But as clever as he was, this time Fischer didn't have an answer.

NINE

It was Thursday morning, and Penny was nervously checking under the van. The old washing-up bowl she'd placed there the previous night had caught quite a bit of oil. She topped it up again. The sooner it was sorted out, the better. She pushed thoughts of the cost to the back of her mind as she got the library ready for the start of the day. Tomorrow was Friday, the start of Penny's weekend. The mobile library only needed to run for one more day, then hopefully Martin would be able to fix her up as good as new.

With Fischer in the front seat, Penny only had to move up to her parking spot by the duck pond. On Thursdays she was in her own village of Cherrytree Downs.

While she set out her camping stuff, Fischer made a bee-line for his favourite tree. She sat back in her chair, a cup of tea in hand, and looked out over the village green. Across the other side was a small row of shops and Mrs Evans was standing in the doorway of her bakery, eating a fresh iced bun.

She waved across to Penny. The baker would have already been at work for hours as everything was made from scratch on the day. The smell of fresh bread and cakes wafting over to her side of the green was too much for Penny to resist, especially since she'd missed breakfast while seeing to the van.

"Fischer," she called, and he came charging over. "You wait in the van for a minute, little man. I'm going across the road to grab a bun. Good boy."

The iced bun was an Evans' bakery special, and she decided to add some rolls to her order as well.

"Morning, Penny, what can I get you?"

"An iced bun and four of your large crusty cheese rolls, please."

Penny's stomach growled audibly with anticipation as Mrs Evans slid the still warm rolls into a paper bag. She patted her pockets and groaned.

"I've left my purse in the van. I'll just go and get it."

Mrs Evans waved away her words. "Don't worry, drop it in next time you're passing."

"I will, thank you."

"So, from what I hear, it was a gangster that killed Robert Reynolds," the woman said, taking a sip of tea from the mug by the till and eying Penny speculatively. She wasn't going to let the amateur sleuth go before she'd shared what she knew.

Penny knew she meant Max Damage. While he obviously wasn't a gangster, he did have a tendency to look and act like one.

"If you mean the musician Max Damage, I don't think he's a gangster, Mrs Evans."

"Well, he has a gang and they've been causing problems all

over the place. Driving too fast, whooping and hollering and making a din. It's shameful. They were in here this morning, as a matter of fact."

"They were up early," Penny said. She had trouble believing a gang of youths would be up much before noon.

"I don't think they'd been to bed yet. They looked shattered, bleary eyed and pale. They were starving, too. Bought every pasty and sausage roll I had in the place. And they just hung around outside, smoking and swearing. I had to ask them to move on several times. Then they left all their rubbish on the pavement, so I had to clean that up. Disgraceful behaviour. PC Bolton would have seen them off. We really could do with a new village bobby if this is the sort we're going to get here in the future."

"I think they were his fans, Mrs Evans, rather than his gang."

"Well, they certainly looked like a gang to me. Who wears a thick black jacket in this beautiful weather?"

"I agree with you. I certainly couldn't do it. I'd be keeling over from heatstroke within the hour. But it's a sort of fan uniform. Oh, I better go, there's a customer at the library." It was Katy Lowry, the barmaid from the Pig and Whistle. "I'll pop in with the money later."

"Tomorrow is fine, dear. I normally see you heading out for your walk on a Friday."

A group of black jacketed youths had pulled up while Penny had been in the bakery. They were sitting on the bonnet of a small red car parked at the side of the green, smoking cigarettes. She saw one young man drop a butt on the floor, grind it in with his heel and leave it while he lit another. Judging by the pile of cigarette ends already littering the ground, they'd been smoking a lot in the short time since they'd arrived.

Penny was furious. They had no clue about how much care the locals took over their village to keep it clean and tidy and a beautiful place for visitors. She dreaded to think about what sort of places they lived in. She made a mental note to go and tidy it up once they'd left.

"They're looking for that rapper Max Damage," Katy said when Penny arrived at the library. "They're all over the area. Some of them are sleeping in the cars in the lay-by on the ring road. Others are on the grass verge with no sleeping bags or tents. Linda Green is doing a roaring trade at her burger van. Obviously, none of them have summer jobs. Or any jobs, for that matter."

"Rain has been forecast for the weekend," Penny said. "Hopefully, they'll all go home when the weather changes."

"They are like a cult following him around. Why did he have to come here?"

"Are they coming into the pub, Katy?"

"The older ones, but the landlord has barred the others. Even if they are old enough to drink, he doesn't want the trouble they'll probably cause. He'll lose the local trade if he lets them in, he knows that. It's not worth a bit of extra money to risk that. Besides, they're probably the sort to get one pint of snakebite and 6 bags of crisps between them."

"I'm glad. I hate to make assumptions about people based on looks, but this crowd unfortunately seem like the sort who would think nothing of getting behind the wheel of a car drunk. They drive dangerously enough as it is. Anyway, enough of them. You've come to look at the books."

As Katy climbed into the van, Penny looked her village with a new eye. It was easy to get complacent when you lived in such idyllic surroundings. She could see Sugar Hill shimmering in the distance beneath the warm, hazy air. A red kite was circling high over Cringle Wood. She could see why Max Damage wanted to come here. He'd come to enjoy the countryside as much as the shoot, hadn't he? Or had he come to get rid of the banker who'd taken control of his music? The idea seemed more than possible. There was a serious amount of money tied to his songs. Max certainly made a big show of being a bit of a thug, but pretending and doing were two different things. However unpleasant he was, she found it hard to believe he was a killer. It seemed more like bravado to her. And of course, he was still here. Only the guilty ran, Penny thought. Or perhaps he was waiting around as a bluff to avoid suspicion falling on him, which it undoubtedly would if he ran.

The gang of Damage fans had finally decided to move on. Far too many of them climbing into the small car to be either safe or legal. They raced off through the village, music blaring, tyres screeching, and headed towards the road that led to Winstoke. A five mile journey along the country roads. Penny prayed there weren't any tractors, wildlife, or walkers in the vicinity.

She waited until they had gone, then grabbed a small dustpan and brush from the van and went to clear up their litter. Cigarette ends, sweet wrappers, and bags from the bakery were swept up and put in the litter bin a few feet away. When Penny returned, Katy had chosen a couple of books. One a fantasy romance and the other filled with recipes.

"Cocktails!" She grinned. "I'm going to try to learn something new for the pub. Who knows when we might get asked for a Singapore Sling or a Long Island Iced Tea? We might even hold a special cocktail night."

"The tea one sounds interesting."

"I'll make you one," Katy said. "You can be my guinea pig. Are you going to the quiz tonight?"

"I wouldn't miss it. Maybe I'll test you and order a cocktail. And knowing Susie, she'll do the same."

The morning passed quickly, with most of her regulars popping in to pick up books and share gossip. In between times it was quiet and peaceful, except for one more shattering squeal as Max Damage's car drove through the village. She noticed the driver and realised it wasn't Max, not because he was without his glasses, but because she was looking for differences, now Susie had told her there was a lookalike.

Moments after the car departed, another smaller vehicle packed to the gills with youngsters in their black jacket uniform sped in its wake. Penny couldn't help but smile, knowing they were on a wild goose chase. But she would be very glad when Max Damage left, one way or another, and all his rabid groupies went home.

She glanced at her watch and stood up.

"Come on, Fish Face, time for a quick walk, then into town."

Penny pulled into the car-park opposite the library and approached the reserved spot. It was only on a Thursday afternoon when she had so many books to swap over that the spot was designated for her. It was clearly marked, yet when she pulled up the space was already taken by a huge black car with tinted windows. It was one of Max Damage's vehicles.

"Oh, for heaven's sake. Just how inconsiderate can you be?"

She sighed and reversed back to the entrance, where she'd spied a space as she entered. It would mean a longer distance carrying the books back and forth to the main library and twice the amount of trips, but there was nothing she could do about it. Whoever was driving the car was nowhere in sight and might not return for hours.

She and Fischer waited to cross the road in front of the main library. She was juggling her phone, her handbag, Fischer's lead and the bag of crusty rolls she was intending to share with her colleagues, when she heard a voice addressing her from behind and her body recoiled in dread.

"Paying their library fines in stale bread rolls, now are they?"

She turned, and with great difficulty plastered a smile on her face. She felt her little dog hide behind her legs.

"Hello, Edward. It's a treat for my colleagues. Freshly baked this morning, actually. How are you?"

"Business is booming. I'm in great demand, as a matter of fact."

Penny recognised the man who stepped up beside Edward, chubby with a florid complexion. It was Samuel Reynolds. His red curly hair was greasy and his small, deep-set eyes bored into hers with unconcealed interest. She noticed the attempt to conceal the cut under his eye with cosmetics had failed miserably. Whatever he'd used was several shades too light compared to the rest of his flushed face. He leered at her, grinning. She felt a shiver of disgust. He slapped Edward on the back.

"You didn't tell me you knew the prettiest lady in town, you old dog."

He obviously hadn't recognised her, Penny thought. Edward blushed but hid his discomfort behind a show of bravado.

"She's the local mobile librarian," Edward said. "How's the old van going? All those penny fines managing to keep you in petrol?"

He exaggerated the word penny and turned to Sammy Reynolds to explain. Both men laughed uproariously while Penny just stood there, feeling slightly nauseous.

"So, what are you doing tonight?" Samuel Reynolds asked her. "Fancy getting a drink with me?"

"Penny is spoken for, Sammy. She's going out with the local Detective Inspector."

"That's right," Penny said, glaring at the man.

The insolent smirk he'd been wearing instantly fell away and some of the colour faded from his blotchy, booze stained face. He jabbed a finger in Penny's face.

"You tell that useless country copper to find the person who shot my brother."

Penny heard Fischer growl low in his throat and bent briefly to pat him. Reassuring him it was okay. Samuel Reynolds continued.

"I saw him running through the smoke. Tell that boyfriend of yours to get off his lazy backside and catch the killer. And you can tell him from me, I'll not rest until they're found. He was within my grasp. I should have tackled him myself. I could have done a better job than these so-called detectives. Useless, the lot of them."

"Detective Inspector Monroe is very good at his job, and is working all hours to find the person responsible," Penny said sharply.

"Well, he really needs to get on with it, Penny," Edward said, laying a calming arm on his companion. "John needs to know who he's dealing with. As his brother's only survivor, Samuel is about to become a very rich man. I'm the one in charge of making all this run smoothly. He's also looking to buy property in the area, Thornehurst Grange as a matter of fact, if we play our cards right. Major Colton is well past his sell by date. It's too much for him to manage. Samuel is going to be a very important person in this community before long, Penny, so I'd not do anything to upset him if I were you. You can pass that onto John when you see him."

Penny felt anger bubble in her stomach and took a deep breath. She had the urge to slap Edward across his stupid, obnoxious face. She was saved by Samuel Reynolds.

"Come on, Ed. Let's go and get a pint," he said, slapping Edward hard enough on the back that he stumbled forward a step. "Your round this time. I'll return the favour once the deal is signed and sealed."

Penny was amused to see Edward squirm. He wasn't the generous type, for one thing. For another, he hated being called Ed.

Samuel Reynolds gave Penny a final glance, running his hand through his hair in what he assumed was a suave, sophisticated move. It was spoiled when the heavy, ornate ring on his index finger caught on a strand and pulled it clean out of his scalp.

Penny turned away. She'd had enough.

"Come on, Fischer. Let's go and see some nice people."

She and Fischer were greeted warmly by Sam and Emma when they entered the library. Penny unhooked Fischer's lead, and he went bounding over, bottom wiggling and claws clicking on the tiles as he greeted them, whining in excitement.

"Hi, you two."

"Hi, Penny. Are you okay?" Emma asked. "You look a bit cross."

Penny pulled a face.

"I'm fine. I just met Edward outside, and someone has taken my parking spot, so the re-stock is going to take twice as long."

"But I put the sign out," Sam said, frowning. "Has it been moved?"

"No, it's still there, Sam," Penny said. "They just chose to ignore it. Either that or they can't read."

"The cheek! I'll give you a hand, Penny. It will be quicker with the two of us and we're quiet at the moment so Emma can cope."

"That's fine," Emma said, nodding. "I get to have little Fischer all to myself."

With Sam helping, the restock was done in no time, but on their last journey the car which had caused all the trouble, decided to leave the car-park in a screech of rubber.

"Typical," Sam said.

Penny laughed. "It's called sod's law, I think, Sam. I'll move the van into my spot now he's gone. Thanks for your help."

"No problem. It saves on the cost of a gym. I'll see you inside. I'll put the kettle on ready."

Back in the library, Penny found her colleagues checking out books for the ladies of the knitting club, but found no sign of Fischer. Sam saw her anxious expression and pointed over to the children's room. Looking through the glass wall, she spied her little dog sitting quietly with the children listening to the storyteller. She grinned and quickly whipping out her phone took a couple of photos.

A moment later, the story was finished and Penny called Fischer back. He made himself comfortable in his bed under the counter while Penny went to make tea. When she returned with the tray, the library was quiet. The children and the storyteller had gone and Fischer was fast asleep.

"Wow, great cheesy rolls," Sam said. "These from Mrs Evans?"

Penny nodded. "I picked them up fresh this morning."

"It must be great working out and about in the villages all week."

"It is. I'm very lucky. Although I've had a few problems with the van. Leaky roof, leaking oil and the engine is having a few problems. I'm afraid the old bus is slowly falling apart."

"Have you been over to Shattock's shop?" Emma asked. "I'm sure he'll have something to help."

"I went in there on Tuesday. He was very helpful, but it needs more than a tube of sealant. His daughter Henri offered to fix up the leaks and the interior problems. Apparently, she's really good at the sort of stuff."

"I nearly knocked her down on Saturday," Emma said. "Just ran across the road from nowhere. Frightened me to death."

"Where was that?" Penny asked.

"On the outskirts of Chiddingborne, just north of Thornehurst. She was in a hurry as well. Looked like she'd run all the way from Cherrytree Downs, right over Sugar Hill, through Rowan Downs and just carried on like she couldn't stop. It was like watching Forrest Gump. I don't know how she manages to walk, let-alone run in those boots she wears. She hardly gave me a second glance when I slammed on the brakes."

"It was that close?" Sam said.

"It was. She's incredibly lucky I wasn't speeding and had a chance to stop in time."

"Was she coming from the direction of the grouse moor, Emma?" Penny asked.

"Yes, I suppose she was coming from that direction."

"And you're absolutely sure it was Henri you saw?"

"Pretty sure, yes. She had on baggy clothes, dark, not like her usual colourful stuff. And she was wearing a hoodie, but I recognised her boots. Why? Do you think she had something to do with what happened at the grange?"

"Possibly. Although I'd appreciate you both keeping quiet for now. I don't want to accuse her of something until I'm positive she was involved."

"Penny Finch, super sleuth, is at it again," Sam said, grinning widely. "Don't worry, we'll keep quiet, won't we, Em?"

"Of course we will."

Penny had more than a sneaking suspicion it had been Henri who'd thrown the smoke bomb. She was easily both clever and capable enough to concoct such a device. Penny shuddered at the thought of how dangerous the girl's actions had been. She finished her roll and her tea and decided to pay a visit to the hardware store. Not for supplies this time, but to have a friendly word with Henrietta Shattock.

TEN

Penny pushed open the door to the hardware shop, rapidly trying to come up with a way to introduce the subject of the smoke bomb. As she entered, she found it was Henri herself who was minding the shop.

The young girl looked up as the bell rang. A smile spreading across her face was quickly replaced by a nervous look as she realised who it was. There must have been something in Penny's visage that said she'd come for more than a box of screws.

"Hi, Penny."

"Hello, Henri. How are you?"

The girl shrugged. "Fine. Can I get you anything?"

"A washing-up bowl, please. I've used mine to catch the oil from a leak under the van."

Henri relaxed a little and moved to the main part of the shop where the bowls were stacked on a shelf.

"Any particular colour?"

"You choose."

Henri picked up a red bowl and moved back behind the counter to the till.

"I saw you at the protest the other day."

Henri turned white and started to shake slightly. Penny hadn't expected her to be so nervous and was beginning to feel guilty about approaching her at all.

"So?"

"It's just a friend said she saw you running across the road at Chiddingborne. She nearly hit you, apparently. You were in such a rush."

"It wasn't me. I was at the protest. Loads of people saw me. But I didn't leave until the trouble started with the Max Damage fans."

Penny nodded and took the bowl, handing over the correct money.

"Right. She must have been mistaken. Thanks for the bowl, Henri. And just so you know, if you need to talk about anything. Anything that's worrying you. I'm here okay?"

Henri avoided her gaze, and it was obvious to Penny she was hiding something. The kinetic ball clock chimed.

"That's closing time. I have to shut the shop now."

Penny stepped outside and Henri locked the door before she'd had a chance to step onto the pavement. A few steps away, she glanced back and saw Henri with her back to the door, hands covering her face and shoulders heaving with sobs. She was about to turn back when the girl stood up, dashed the tears from her face and marched across the shop floor. She disappeared behind the curtain into a room beyond.

Driving out of Winstoke on her way home, Penny couldn't help thinking about Henri Shattock.

"I think I made a real mess of that, Fischer. She obviously grasps the fact I know something. She's going to be worried sick now that I'll tell someone. John maybe? And he's the police. She's got a secret, Fish Face, and it's terrifying her. It was obvious when she came to the library the other day that she had something on her mind she wanted to talk about. I should have sat her down and insisted there and then that she tell me. But what good would it have done? She wasn't ready. I'd have frightened her even more than she already is."

Penny hoped it was only the bomb that Henri was involved in and not the death of Robert Reynolds. She slowed down at the junction to Rowan Downs, checking for traffic. She could see Chips Ahoy, the fish and chip shop on one side, and the old cottage on the other, but there wasn't another car in sight. She was just pulling out when someone eating a bag of chips walked right in front of the van. She slammed on the brakes, heart hammering in her chest. She recognised him instantly. It was Max Damage.

The musician stopped dead in his tracks and turned to face the van, eyes filled with fury. She checked the mirrors and when she was sure the road was clear, pulled on the handbrake and got out of the van.

"What the hell were you thinking?" He spat. "You could have killed me. Why don't you watch where you're going?"

"I was watching exactly where I was going, Mr Damage. If I hadn't had been, then you wouldn't be standing here shouting at me now. And while we are on the subject, I've just about had enough of your rude behaviour. This is the second time this week you've bumped into me and hurled abuse for something that was your fault and I'm not standing for it anymore."

Max was taken aback by her tone. In fact, Penny was pretty amazed at it herself. He stared at her. He obviously wasn't used to people answering back.

"I did look," he said sulkily. He squinted at the library. "Your van is green. Everything is green around here. It all looks the same."

Penny nearly laughed. "Yes, it's called the countryside. If you hate it so much, then why are you still here?"

"Because until this stupid police investigation is over, I'm not allowed to leave. Besides, that peasant Reynolds is about to steal my music and I have to be here for the will reading at the grange on Saturday. Not that it's any of your business."

"He's stolen your music? How?" Penny asked, knowing full well this was the case from what Susie had told her.

"An oversight in the paperwork. You can't trust anyone nowadays. He told me I could have them over his dead body. I call that a verbal agreement, don't you? I'd kill to get the rights back, but honestly, my new stuff is much better. My new tracks are going to blow the download charts off the net. Just you wait and see."

A car pulled up alongside them, braking hard. The driver wound down his window. Penny was amazed at how much he looked like the singer.

"I've given that fan car the slip for now, Max. But they'll be back. We'd better go."

Max Damage threw the almost full bag of chips in the gutter and jumped into the vehicle. The tyres screeched as it turned onto the road towards Chiddingborne.

Penny sighed and picked up the discarded food. She jogged across the road to the chip shop and deposited them in the bin before returning to her van. Fischer gave her a look.

"I know, Fish Face. Rude, boorish and uncivilised. All that education and wealth, and he's nothing but a greedy, selfish idiot."

She wondered if Max realised what he'd said had moved him to the top of her suspect list?

Penny turned towards home from the junction and heard the revving of an engine behind her. It was a small red car, moving erratically and far too fast. The brakes squealed in the road and it almost hit the back bumper of the van.

The horn started blaring and a youth in a puffer jacket wound down his window and started hurling abuse. Telling her to get a move on. Penny checked her speedometer and noticed she was driving two miles an hour over the speed limit. She touched the brake and slowed down a fraction. Her heart was pounding, but she refused to be intimidated.

"The sooner these hoodlums leave this area, the better," she told her little dog. "Good job he can't be in two places at once. When he's gone, things will calm down and our little villages will be back to normal."

The small car raced past Penny, the driver leaning on the horn.

She reached her village and pulled up outside her cottage.

"Thank goodness we're home, Fischer."

She slid the washing-up bowl under the oil leak and

standing up saw John Monroe outside the police house. He was in shirtsleeves, his tie loose around his neck. As per normal, his phone was glued to his ear. He gave her a wave as he concluded the conversation. She put Fischer in the house and walked over.

"Hi, John. Finished early today?"

Monroe slipped his phone into his pocket.

"I'm on call still. Literally, as my phone has never stopped since I got here. I was brushing up on a bit of trivia for tonight's quiz and trying to unpack a few boxes."

He glanced down the road as though looking for something.

"Is everything all right?" Penny asked, following his gaze, but seeing nothing out of the ordinary.

Monroe shook his head. "Kids racing through the village. I've called it in just now. They've already been given a warning once this week. That was their last chance. It was very nearly a disaster. Susie and her children were about to cross the road when it came tearing through the village. They missed her by an inch. It was only her quick thinking that stopped them from being hit. My heart was in my mouth. There was nothing I could do."

"Oh no. Are they all right?"

"They're fine. A bit shaken up, Susie more than the kids, but she calmed down. She's furious. No doubt they'll be a piece in the paper about it soon."

"They're chasing after Max Damage. They're an absolute menace, John."

"Yes, I know. I'll be having a word with him as well. I'm giving serious thought to putting him under house arrest or something at the grange to stop him moving about. But he seems to be all over the place. I can't pin him down."

Penny was about to bring him up to date on what she'd learned so far when his phone rang again. He snatched it up.

"Pull them in for a warning and go over that car with a fine-tooth comb. MOT. Tax. Insurance, driver's license. Breathalyser. The works. If there's so much as a cracked indicator light, I want that car seized and the kids sent on their way with a severe warning at the very least."

The conversation didn't seem to be ending, so Penny mouthed 'see you later,' and waved when he nodded. Setting back off to her cottage.

"It's quiz time, Fischer," Penny said, clipping on his lead. He'd been standing at the door for the last ten minutes, knowing somehow it was the night they went to the pub. She'd heard plenty of stories about dogs knowing what time it was, Fischer was the same, particularly when it came to walks or food, but days of the weeks was a new one on her.

Penny arrived a few minutes later than normal, having stopped for Fischer to visit his favourite tree. He'd found an enticing smell and wouldn't leave until he'd explored all traces of it.

She glanced around as she headed to the bar but could see no sign of either of her teammates.

"Hi, Penny. So, ready for that cocktail?" Katy said, smiling. "I'll make you that Long Island Iced Tea if you like? I've been practicing."

Penny just fancied a glass of fruit juice if she was honest, but Katy looked so keen to show off her new skills she found herself nodding.

She glanced round for Susie. The table they normally sat at by the fireplace was already taken by a casual team who just turned up occasionally. They weren't regulars. Susie hadn't arrived.

She turned back, eyes widening as she watched Katy add various shots to the glass. Gin, vodka, white rum, tequila, triple sec, cola, some sort of syrup and finally a splash of lemon juice. She'd been drawn to the word 'tea' in the name, but this was going to taste nothing like tea. It was also going to be far more expensive than her usual brew.

"I did mention to them that your team sits there, by the way," Katy said, nodding over to the fireplace. "But they sat there, anyway."

"It's okay, I'll sit in the window."

"Ta da!" Katy said, throwing in a stirrer, a pink paper umbrella, a slice of lemon on the edge of the glass and a cherry on a cocktail stick. "What do you think?"

Penny took a sip. It was rich and sweet and had enough alcohol it in to last a week.

"Wowsers! It's strong. And sweet. But quite nice, actually. Thanks Katy."

She carried her drink to the window seat, where Fischer made himself comfortable under the table and saw John walking over the road. He gave her a wave. She could see Katy had already started pulling him his usual, a Guinness, and he arrived at the table with a pint flourishing a perfect shamrock pattern in the creamy head.

"That looks a bit posh," Penny said. "Katy's upping her game."

"Not as posh as yours," John replied. "What on earth are you drinking? I assume there is something to drink in among all that stuff?"

Penny told him and pushed the drink over for him to try.

"Good grief! That's... actually, I don't even know where to start. Rather you than me. I'll stick with my black liquid gold. Thank you very much."

He reached down and scratched Fischer's ears, eliciting a happy little whine from the canine, whose tail had been thumping on the table leg ever since John had walked in.

"No Susie tonight?" he asked.

"No, which is worrying. If she wasn't coming, she'd have sent me a text. I hope she's all right after that near accident."

"She was, honestly. And if you haven't heard from her, she's probably just running late. Ah, I believe we're about to start."

The sheet for the picture round a bit later was placed on the table. John was team Agatha Quiztee's specialist at the picture round, but for some reason he was taking no notice, just staring into space. Penny was about to nudge him when the pub door opened and Susie walked in. She had her head down, eyes locked on her phone screen. Penny watched as she sauntered over to the table at the fireplace. She was about to sit down when she noticed a sea of strange faces grinning at her. She laughed and apologised, then looked up to find Penny frantically waving at her from the window seat.

She indicated she'd be a minute, went to the bar and brought back her usual glass of wine. Obviously, a cocktail wasn't on the cards tonight.

"Hi you two. Sorry I'm late."

"Are you and the kids okay, Susie? John told me about the near miss with Max Damage's fan car."

"We're all fine, Penny. I'm furious, though. There will be a scathing report in the paper about them."

She put the phone on the table but constantly kept looking at it. A moment later, it pinged, and she snatched it up with eager anticipation. Penny glanced at John to see if he'd noticed, but he was sipping his pint and still staring into space.

Round one was Penny's favourite. Literature. If she didn't know the answer immediately, she found she could always puzzle it out. One such question was on tonight's list. She concentrated on trying to pull forth that extra clue she needed. She looked at her team mates, both of whom usually fed her relevant bits of information to help her find the answer, but they were both miles away. Susie glanced up briefly, smiled and nodded, then was glued to her phone again, thumbs flashing over the screen as she answered a message.

Penny stared at them both. She may as well be on her own for all the assistance and company these two were tonight. The quiz master announced the last question for the round and she was suddenly aware she'd missed the previous three. She quickly jotted down an answer she was sure was wrong, but it was better than nothing.

Then came the picture round. She pushed the sheet under John's hand and gave him the pen. He looked down absent-mindedly and scribbled answers beneath the images, not once conferring with her or Susie. Not that Susie would have been of any use.

Penny looked at what he'd written. His normally neat handwriting was little more than scribbles. No one would ever work out what he meant by these in order to mark them. There was one she knew was wrong.

"Are you sure this one is right, John?"

"Mmm? Oh, maybe not."

"Isn't it Versailles?"

"Yes. You're right, it is. My mistake. Well done."

At the half time interval, John went up to the bar for another pint. Susie said yes to another wine, but Penny was still struggling with her cocktail.

"You've been quiet," Penny said to Susie once John had left. "Is everything all right?" she leaned closer. "You've been messing with your phone all night. I'm surprised you managed to drink your wine."

Susie looked up and smiled. A half smile of someone preoccupied, a little unsure and, to Penny's mind, nervous. Which was very strange.

"I'm sorry, Penny. I'm all over the place tonight. I've not been much help, have I?"

"You've not been any help at all, frankly. But it doesn't matter, we've probably forfeited this match, anyway. Phones aren't allowed. So what's going on? Are the kids okay? Is it your parents? James? Come on, Susie, I know something's going on. Is it work?"

Susie pointed to her phone. "It's work. Something I'm, um, researching. I can't tell you about it yet." She tucked her phone away for the first time that evening, perhaps worried that something on there would give her secret away.

Now Penny was concerned. In all their years of friendship,

right from being tiny kids at first school, she and Susie had shared all their secrets and kept them.

"What is it, Susie? I can see something is going on. Tell me."

"Honestly, it's nothing, Penny. I'm just being silly. A silly old fool."

"For goodness' sake, just spill the beans, will you? I'll get it out of you eventually, you know I will. Just rip off the plaster now and tell me. I'll keep mum. I always do, don't I?"

"It is work, well actually it's someone at work. His name is Tom."

"Oh," a smile spread over Penny's face. Concern was replaced by relief and happiness for her friend.

She deserved it. She remembered vividly the pits of despair Susie had fallen into when her husband had left her for another woman. She had rallied for her children's sake more than her own and had maintained both dignity and strength as she strived to ensure the kids had a balanced relationship with both their parents. In the aftermath of the breakup, Susie had worked tirelessly, working her way up from junior reporter and general dogsbody, to finally take her current position at the paper. She'd worked hard and deserved the recognition and promotion. But Penny sensed there was still something Susie wasn't telling her.

"Do the children know?"

"No. That's part of the problem. I don't know what to do. Should I be in a relationship at all? My focus should be on the children. They come first. What will they think if I'm in a relationship with someone who isn't their father?"

"Well, what do they think about their father being with

someone who isn't you? Come on, Susie, you're allowed to be happy. I'm sure when they meet him, they'll think he's wonderful."

Susie shrank in her seat.

"He is wonderful, isn't he?"

Penny fixed her with a look. She needed more information.

"He's young," Susie said finally.

Penny was a little surprised. What did Susie mean by 'young?' She had no chance to ask as John returned. Susie thanked him and proceeded to answer yet another message. John smiled at her, asked if she was okay, then did the same. Penny was sitting with two of the people she was closest to, yet she'd never felt more alone. This quiz night was definitely a bust. By the time the last round came, they'd hadn't even answered half the questions. She threw the pen down. It was pointless continuing. She couldn't hope to win on her own. When the results were announced, Agatha Quiztee came last.

Susie finished her wine quickly as her phone chirped with another message. She stood up.

"I'm going to head off."

"Yes, me too," John said. "I haven't even put the sheets on the bed in the house yet. I don't know which box they're in. Are you ready, Penny? I'll walk you home."

"Actually, I haven't finished my drink. You two go on ahead. I'll be fine."

Monroe appeared torn between walking Susie home and leaving Penny alone in the pub. Susie made it easy for him.

"I don't need you to walk me home tonight." She jiggled her phone at Penny. "I'm getting a lift."

"You only live across the other side of the village. It's not worth the taxi fare," John said.

"It's not a taxi," Susie said, grinning. She bent to give Penny a farewell hug, then cheerily said goodbye and left.

"She'll be fine, John. I don't mind if you want to leave as well. It's not as though you've really been here tonight, anyway."

"I'm so sorry, Penny," he said, putting his arm around her shoulders and pulling her close. He kissed the top of head. Resting his lips there for a moment before leaning back. "It's this blasted case. I thought I could at least switch off for a couple of hours and enjoy the quiz, but my brain just won't stop working. We've done a huge amount of work in the background: fingertip searches, suspect and witness interviews, forensic analysis, you name it. But we're no further forward. I've been living off hastily eaten sandwiches and copious amounts of disgusting coffee just to keep awake. This is the stuff that goes on in the background that the general public doesn't see. It's utterly exhausting."

"Did you get the results back from the gun Fischer found?"

John nodded. "It was the one Robert Reynolds was using. Unfortunately, the only fingerprints on it were his own."

"Surely he didn't shoot himself?"

"Not without some very inventive thinking. It's almost impossible to kill yourself with a shotgun because the barrel is too long for you to reach the trigger yourself."

John sighed and rubbed his eyes.

"You need a holiday, John. You'll run yourself into an early grave if you keep this up. It's not healthy."

"I agree with you there. Unfortunately, until this case is solved, all leave is cancelled."

"What about afterwards? Let's take a week off somewhere and relax. What do you think?"

John grinned. "Now, that is an excellent idea. It will give me something good to look forward to. As well as a goal to get this case solved more quickly. Not that I can do anything faster than I am. But you never know, I might get a second wind or that one clue which suddenly breaks the case wide open, as the cliche goes."

"I'm sure you will. Come on, you can walk me home."

"Gladly. But please, let's not discuss the case. I'm sick to death of thinking about it. I need to clear my brain completely so I can think afresh."

ELEVEN

The alarm went off, jarring Penny awake from an alcohol in-duced sleep. It was Friday, and she had no need to get up, but she'd forgotten to turn off the alarm when she'd got home the night before. She turned it off now, trying not to move her head too much as it was pounding. She'd only drunk three quarters of the cocktail, but that was enough.

"Never again," she muttered into her pillow. She turned as her little dog belly crawled up the covers and licked her face. "Go and put the kettle on, Fish Face." He crawled closer, his little wet nose touching hers. She scratched his ears. "Okay, I'll do it."

She ventured downstairs gingerly, trying not to throw up. It wasn't a hangover as such, but the headache brought on by the mix of so many different spirits. She needed painkillers be-fore it turned into a full-blown migraine, ruining her day off.

She let Fischer out into the garden, put the kettle on, then swilled down a couple of maximum strength tablets with a glass of water. Hopefully, they'd work fast. She couldn't remember the last time she felt so poorly.

With a cup of tea and a couple of slices of toast in her system, an hour later, Penny began to feel human enough to get showered and dressed. Her thoughts swirled with a combination of the case, John and Susie's new young friend. She would have loved to meet up with Susie and find out all about Tom, but unlike Penny, Susie was at work.

Downstairs, feeling almost back to normal, she found Fischer at the door, patiently waiting with his lead in his mouth.

The day was warm, with bright sunshine in a blue sky. She dropped in to give Mrs Evans the money she owed her, then decided she'd walk along the chalk stream for a change. The water was sparkling and so clear you could see to the colourful stones on the bottom, and watch the little fish darting in and out of the river water crowfoot and starworts. Along the edges of the low bank grew watercress and lesser water-parsnip. She grabbed Fischer's collar and crouched down, telling him to be quiet as she saw movement in the foliage across on the opposite bank. A second later, she was rewarded by the appearance of a sleek head, followed by a sleeker body. An otter. Fischer was stock still, watching the creature intently. It was the first time he'd seen one. A moment later, it slipped silently into the water and disappeared downstream.

"Good boy, Fischer."

Up on Sugar Hill, the suffocating heat of the day was ameliorated by the breeze that blew over the top. Penny scared a grouse as she walked. It fluttered ungainly into the air, flying a short distance before coming to land in a patch of thick coarse grass. Once again, perfectly camouflaged.

She sat down at the top and took in the view while Fischer snuffled happily in the undergrowth and, bringing out a small flask of tea and a cheese scone from her pocket, had an impromptu picnic. The fresh air and additional sustenance were exactly what was needed to clear away the last vestiges of her headache.

She smiled, thinking back to her declaration she and John should take a holiday when the case was over. This was next level relationship stuff, and they'd hardly got past the first. She'd surprised herself when she'd suggested it. It was definitely the alcohol that was to blame. But John had been all for it, going so far as to mention going up to the Peak District where he was from. He'd said Fischer would adore all the walks up there and she'd loved the fact he'd assumed the little dog would be going too. It just seemed so natural.

She leaned back, feeling content and immensely happy. She was looking forward to her future with this man.

As early as she could on Saturday morning, Penny drove the van over to Martin's garage. He was waiting for her.

"Thanks, Martin, you're a lifesaver."

"Anytime. Hopefully, it's an easy fix. I'll give you a ring later and let you know."

Back at home, she opened the door for Fischer to go in and out as he pleased and started to tidy up. She'd made good headway when her phone pinged. It was Susie texting to see if she and the children could come over? Penny immediately suggested they come for lunch.

"I'll bring dessert," was Susie's reply.

It didn't take long for her to throw together a green salad with grated beetroot, carrot and cherry tomatoes off the vine. A potato salad with her own dressing, a large multi seed loaf from the freezer and a large vegetarian quiche were the final dishes. She'd just finished washing up when the doorbell went.

Soon they were all seated at the garden table in the warm sunshine, tucking in happily. Billy and Ellen were chattering ten to the dozen, bringing her up to date with what had happened at school and all the things they were doing during the summer holidays. After dessert, a large strawberry cheesecake courtesy of Mrs Evans, the children went to play in the garden with Fischer while Penny and Susie chatted over a pot of tea.

"So, do you want to tell me about Tom?" Penny asked.

"I don't even know where to start. You know I'd been with James for so long I didn't even realise Tom was flirting with me until one of the secretaries told me. You could have knocked me down with a feather. How could I not recognise it?"

"I didn't realise John was interested to start with either. There's nothing unusual in that."

"But John isn't twenty-four, Penny."

"Twenty-four?"

"I know. It dawned on me this morning that the age difference between me and Tom is practically the same as between Tom and my son. It was a sobering thought."

"Well, I'll admit I wasn't expecting him to be that young, but I saw you at the pub on Thursday, Susie. You were like a schoolgirl in the throes of her first crush."

"Oh, don't, Penny. I feel ridiculous enough as it is."

"I don't mean it that way. What is obvious is how he makes you feel. Wanted and attractive and young. You're all of those things, Susie. You just don't see it yourself."

"So you think I should carry on with it, then?" Penny smiled and shook her head. "How am I supposed to answer that, Susie? I haven't even met him. But I'll tell you one thing: if you don't grasp opportunities now, when will you? I mean, look what happened between Edward and me. I wasted so many years of my life with him being unhappy. I don't want you to do the same. James did more than just leave you for someone else, Susie. He crushed your belief in yourself. Tom is obviously bringing that feeling of self-worth back. Whether it turns out to be nothing more than a brief dalliance, a bit of a mutual flirtation with no strings attached, then who am I to say it's wrong? We might both be close to forty, but that doesn't mean we're no longer capable of feeling young and having fun."

"But what about the kids? My priority is them, Penny."

"Of course it is, that's the way it should be, but you can have both, can't you? As long as you're careful and take it slowly, there's no reason why Billy and Ellen wouldn't come to like him as much as you obviously do. But, as I've just said, if you think it's just a bit of a fling, then make the most of it behind the scenes to start with and see how it progresses. I assume he knows you have children?"

"Yes, and he seems fine with it."

"But?"

"But it's early days and I'm not sure he's thinking far enough ahead. He's too young to be saddled with a middle-aged divorcee with two children, Penny."

"Then you've answered your own question. But you're not defined by labels, Susie. You're not just a divorcee, not just a mother, you're Susie Hughes, who happens to have two fantastic kids but is no longer married to their father. If you want my honest opinion, you're rushing into this far too fast. Tom might not be thinking that far ahead, and in that I agree with him, but you're thinking so far into the future that you're at risk of ruining what you have in the present. Take it one day at a time, Susie. It will evolve one way or another, and in the meantime, you can have some fun. You deserve it."

"So basically you're saying live in the moment?"

Penny nodded. "I suppose I am. I know it's difficult when you're not just responsible for yourself. But what's the point in worrying about a future that hasn't happened yet?"

Susie leaned over and gave her friend a fierce hug.

"Thank you for talking me off the ledge, Penny. You always make so much sense. I knew there was a reason I chose you to be my best friend in infant school."

"I think it was the other way around, actually," Penny said.

A few minutes after Susie and the children had left, there was a knock at the door.

"Susie must have forgotten something," she said to Fischer as she answered it.

But it wasn't Susie, it was Henrietta Shattock.

"I did it," Miss Finch, she said in floods of tears. "I killed that man."

Penny took the trembling girl into the kitchen where she sat her at the table and poured her a glass of juice. She busied herself making a pot of tea while Henri absently stroked Fischer's head. By some sixth sense he'd understood Henri was upset so had rested his head on her knee. Comforting the girl in the only way he knew how. Penny smiled. Who could resist those soulful brown eyes?

"You do understand the seriousness of what you're telling me, Henri?" Penny said gently.

The girl nodded. "I know. I have to tell someone, but I'm scared." Her voice broke, and she started to cry, hiccuping through the sobs. "I can't tell dad. He'll be so disappointed in me. And I can't go to the police, I'm too afraid. I don't want to be arrested. I just need someone to help me. Tell me what to do. You've always been really kind, especially since mum died. Will you help me? Please? I just want to do the right thing. I can't keep it a secret anymore. It's making me sick."

"Of course I'll help you, Henri. Can you tell me what happened? From the beginning? How did you get your hands on a gun?"

"I made it," she said simply. "It's not hard. We sell everything I needed at the shop. And I used the fertiliser from Pike's farm for the explosives. When it was finished, I hid it at the edge of the moor, ready for when I needed it."

"And you made the smoke bomb, too?" Henri nodded and sniffed. Penny went to retrieve a roll of kitchen paper and handed it to the girl. "What happened next?"

"I waited until I saw Robert Reynolds walking over the moor, then collected the gun from where I'd hidden it, then I threw the smoke bomb. Once it was thick enough, I ran over and pointed the gun at him, but he saw me and turned. It was awful, he looked so scared. I changed my mind, Penny. Honestly I did. I couldn't do it. I decided to run away, but I tripped and stumbled and the gun went off and I must have shot him! It was horrible. I wish I hadn't done it. I froze and just laid there for a bit. Then I ran and hid in the hedge. I was sick. But I couldn't let anyone find me, otherwise they'd know it was me. So I took off again. I couldn't stop. I just ran and ran. I just had to get away from there."

She was sobbing uncontrollably now, and Penny put her arms around her and held her close until she had no more tears left.

"Here, Henri, have a drink. I know this is difficult, but you're doing so well. It's the right thing to do, telling me what happened. We'll sort it out, Henri. Can you tell me why you wanted to shoot Robert Reynolds?"

"Because he ruined my family. My dad would be happy and my mum would still be alive if it wasn't for him. I hated him."

"You're talking about the farm?"

Henri nodded. "He had some scheme and persuaded dad to invest in it. He didn't even live here anymore, but came to visit. I was only young, but I remember hearing mum say afterwards she thought it was a mistake. But Reynolds had talked dad into it and something went wrong. We lost the farm and not longer after mum died. It was all his fault."

Penny's mind was whirling while she listened to the girl. She'd been thinking about the murder since the day it happened, trying to fit all the disparate and seemingly unrelated pieces together in an attempt to make the whole picture. She was almost there, she was sure of it.

"How did you know Robert Reynolds was going to be at the shoot, Henri?"

"I saw him when I was at the protest last year. They talked about the shoot a lot at Pike's farm. They were the ones raising the birds, and it made them a lot of money. I heard them talking about him, saying he was there every year. He never missed it. I planned it for months, Penny. Oh god, what have I done? They're going to lock me up, aren't they? I don't want to go to prison! What will my dad do without me?"

She suddenly bolted upright in a panic, looking for a way to escape. Penny took her by the shoulders and held her.

"I'm not going to lie to you, Henri. It's a shock that you've been planning this for months. However, I do understand why you thought you needed to get revenge. But, listen to me, you changed your mind at the last minute. When it came right down to the final moment, Henri, you couldn't do it. That's what we need to hold on to. What did you do with the gun you made?"

"I took it apart and put everything back where I found it. It's not a gun anymore."

"Okay. I have one final question for you. What did you use for the ammunition?"

"The little lead weights we sold in the shop for fishing flies. I filled the cartridges with them."

Penny thought back to how many shots she'd actually heard that day. There were four dead grouse, but she definitely hadn't heard four shots. So how could four birds and one man have been killed when she'd only heard, at most, three shots?

"Of course!"

"What is it?" Henri asked.

"I don't think you killed Robert Reynolds, Henri."

"I did. Haven't you been listening?"

"I have. Every word, and I know you aren't responsible for his death. Listen..."

Penny sat Henri down and told her step-by-step exactly what she thought had happened. Henri stared wide-eyed and open-mouthed as what Penny was telling her slowly sank in. When she'd finished, Penny took out her phone.

"I need to call John Monroe, Henri, all right? I need to tell him what we know."

Henri nodded.

"Good girl."

Penny rang John's number, but it went straight to voicemail so she tried Winstoke police station.

"Hi, it's Penny Finch. I'm trying to get hold of DI Monroe. Is he there?"

"I'm sorry, Penny," the desk sergeant said. "He's over at Thornehurst Grange. Can I pass on a message?"

"No, don't worry. I'll head over there. Thanks."

"We need to go over to the grange, Henri."

"Do we have to?" she asked in a small voice.

"I'm sorry, sweetheart, but it's the only way. It's not going to be easy, but stay strong, okay? I'll be with you all the time, but I need to tell John what actually happened. And I'll need to use your van as mine's in the garage."

"But you're not insured."

Penny smiled. "I think that's the least of our problems, don't you? Besides, I know a friendly policeman."

TWELVE

Due to the urgency of their journey, Penny was tempted to put her foot down on the drive over to Thornehurst Grange, but the last thing she needed was an accident. Henri was right. She wasn't insured to drive Shattock's van, but she could see the girl shaking in the seat beside her and knew she was in no fit state to get behind the wheel. She also didn't want to run the risk of Henri changing her mind and suddenly deciding to drive off in the opposite direction.

It was strange driving these roads without her little four-legged friend beside her, but it was safer for him to remain at home. She had no idea of the welcome she'd receive when she got to the grange. It could prove to be dangerous because she was about to unmask a killer. She'd sent a text to her mum, letting her know Fischer was at the house on his own. No doubt Sheila would be over there now, either keeping him company or taking him back to her own house until Penny returned. He'd probably have learned several new tricks by the time she got back.

The protesters and the Max Damage fans were still out in force when she arrived at the road entrance. There was a healthy uniformed police presence this time, and they were managing to keep the two factions apart successfully.

At the iron gates leading to the estate, she was stopped by a constable. She wound down her window.

"Are you expected?"

"Not exactly, but I have important information about the murder. My name is Penny Finch." "

"That's fine, Miss Finch, you're on the list."

He waved at a guard on the gate who opened them. She drove through. On the list? Penny thought. What list? Someone at the station must have called John and told him I'd rung.

She glanced at the girl next to her. Henri had sunk so low in the seat she was barely visible above the window ledge.

"How are you doing, Henri?"

"I feel sick."

"It will be over soon."

Penny pulled up and parked next to John's car. Major Colton was on the doorstep waiting for her. Her imminent arrival had obviously been announced from the gate.

"Hello, Penny."

"Major Colton. We're here to see DI Monroe. I believe he's here?"

The Major eyed Henri but said nothing.

"Yes, he's in the billiard room with the others. You know the way I think?"

"I do. Thank you Major. Come on, Henri."

If you didn't know where you were going, it was easy to get lost in the maze of hallways inside the grange. The large drawing room to the left had its doors wide open, and Penny saw several men and women dressed in country outfits. More guests waiting to be allowed to get out on the moor.

Further down the hall, she heard voices coming from the billiard room. Again the door was wide open so Penny, followed by an increasingly reluctant Henri, walked straight in.

The room was straight out of an Agatha Christie novel. Oak panelled with a full size billiard table in the centre. A long green shade hung over the centre and cue racks and an antique scoreboard hung on the wall. At the far end of the room were three large green leather Chesterfield settees surrounding a coffee table. And a bar in the corner displayed numerous bottles of spirits in a glass cabinet. Penny gulped nervously as she realised what was about to happen. Just like in a novel, she was about to unmask the killer with all the suspects gathered together in a country house. If it wasn't so serious, she might have laughed.

Sitting at the table were Samuel Reynolds and Max Damage. Standing before them was John Monroe, holding a shotgun. He turned as Penny and Henri crossed the room, their shoes squeaking on the parquet floor.

"Penny. I heard you were on your way over. What are you doing here?"

"Could I have a word?"

"Yes, of course."

She moved over to a quiet corner with Henri, and John followed.

"What's going on, Penny. And who is this?"

"This is Henri, John. She's come to me with some important news."

Penny told John everything she knew, including how she'd come to work out who the murderer was.

"Good grief. I think you might be right, Penny."

"I know I am, John. It couldn't have been any other way. But I'm concerned about, Henri."

"Well, Henri," John said gently. "I can't pretend that what you did won't have repercussions, but I'll do my best to see you're dealt with fairly. That's all I can say for now, until I've heard what Penny has to tell us. All right?" The young girl nodded. "Penny, what do you want to do? No, don't tell me. You want to do a 'Poirot.' Am I right?"

"Well, I suppose so, yes. I've got it all straight in my head, you see. And it might be best if you're concentrating on the murderer while I'm speaking. That way, if anything should happen, you'll be able to stop it. Forewarned and all that."

"What's going on?" Max shouted.

John glanced at him, then back to Penny. "All right, the floor is all yours. Henri, perhaps you could take a seat on the other side of the billiard table, out of the way?"

Henri nodded and did as she was told.

"Whose gun is that, John?"

John lifted his hand. "Sammy Reynolds'. It's been cleared as the murder weapon. I was just about to give it back to him."

"Is it loaded?"

"No, of course not."

"Okay, good. Well, here goes."

Penny took a deep breath and walked to the middle of the room.

"Mr Reynolds," John began. "As I was saying, your gun has been tested and is not the murder weapon, so I am returning it to you as promised."

"About time. I told you it wasn't," Sammy said. Snatching the shotgun from John's outstretched hand.

"Now, I believe Miss Finch has some news about the case. Go on, Penny. We're listening."

Penny suddenly felt a rush of nerves. Every eye in the room was on her. Had she got it wrong? It had been a confusing case, but she had picked apart every clue and put it back together in the only way possible. No, she was right. She knew exactly who the killer was. She took a deep breath.

"Henri Shattock came to me this afternoon in order to confess," she began.

"I knew it!" Sammy suddenly blurted out. "She's the one who threw the smoke bomb and used it to cover up the murder. I saw her running away. I demand you arrest her. Go on, what are you waiting for?"

"I suggest you calm down, Mr Reynolds," John said. Steel in his voice. "I don't believe Miss Finch has finished. And I, for one, would like to hear what she has to say."

"Thank you, Detective Inspector," Penny said. "Henri is a very gifted young woman with an extraordinary talent for making things. But she used her talent for wrong when she made a gun, powered by nitrogen fertiliser as an explosive, to shoot a handful of lead shot. In short, she made a shotgun."

"Cor," Max Damage said. The tone of admiration in his voice was unmistakable.

"But, talented as she is," Penny continued. "She has no experience with firearms and the gun she made didn't have the power needed in order to shoot and kill Robert Reynolds. Yes, the gun was fired, but by accident..."

"A likely story," Sammy said. John growled.

"The gun was fired," Penny repeated. "By accident as Henri tripped in her hurry to get away. But the shot itself never reached Mr Reynolds. The lead fell short and landed where my dog found it. You see, the type of lead Henri added to the gun cartridges is actually used for fly-fishing to weight the flies. With the typical groove manufactured in each ball, it couldn't have been propelled far enough to hit the target. He was simply too far away. It was an incredibly foolish thing to do, but Henri Shattock is not responsible for the death of Robert Reynolds."

"Rubbish," Sammy spat. "She admitted she made a gun to shoot him with! I demand you arrest her, Monroe. She made a smoke bomb, she built a gun and was on the moor, intending to shoot my brother. She's confessed! What more evidence do you need?"

"More than this, Reynolds. And if you don't be quiet, I'll arrest you for obstruction. Now, shut up and sit down! Penny, was there anything else?"

"Yes. The first thing that bothered me was the four dead grouse. How were they killed? There certainly weren't enough shots fired that morning to kill four birds and one man. I only heard three shots. So how did they die? And why had they been arranged so neatly? They were all in a very neat line, side-by-side. It was obvious to me that these birds had been killed prior to the first party going out onto the moor."

"Maybe they were from an old shoot," Max Damage said.

"Nobody would leave the birds. That's the whole point of the shoot, isn't it? To see how many you can kill so you can come back to show off your achievement? They would then be sent down to the kitchen. Nothing wasted in the country, Mr Damage. Besides, if they had been left, then they wouldn't have lasted long. They'd have been eaten by predators the first night. No, these birds were freshly killed that morning. I believe if someone questions the Pikes at the farm, they'll find they were from there, and they were paid well to supply them and keep their mouths shut."

"But why would they leave them on the moor?" John asked.

"They were put there deliberately for one person to find. But it wasn't the Pikes who did it. Isn't that right, Max? Or should I say, Mr Maximilian Theodore Cavendish III?"

Max Damage laughed, but there was no humor in it. "Oh, man. Lady, you are out of your mind. None of that is true. Why would I need someone to leave birds for me when I was out with my own gun, ready to shoot them?"

"Because you can't see, Max. You need to wear glasses because of laser eye surgery, which unfortunately went wrong. You couldn't have even seen a bird without them let-alone shoot one, and I know you weren't wearing them on the day."

Max Damage glared at Penny but said nothing.

"Is this true?" John said.

"Yeah, yeah, so what? I wear glasses. Happy now?"

"So, who brought the birds?" John asked Penny.

"Max has a driver who is a dead ringer for him. It's how he's managed to stay ahead of his fans, and appear to be in two places at once. I think you'll find it was him who shot and collected the birds from Pike's farm and left them for Max in a prearranged place to pick up on the way back after the shoot. Making it appear as though he'd shot them. It's all to do with his public image. Being blind as a bat and having to wear glasses with thick prescription lenses is not great for his brand."

"Fine! You're right," Max said. "I had the grouse placed there by my driver that morning because I'd never be able to see the damn things. There's no law against it."

"And that's what made me realise you couldn't have shot Reynolds unless you'd been right on top of him. But you weren't. You were separated by the smoke bomb that Henri had let off."

"This is all speculative nonsense," Sammy said, getting up. "No one knows what happened out there. It was thick with smoke."

"I do," said Penny. "It was you who killed your brother. Your motive is one as old as the hills. Money. It was greed, pure and simple."

"Utter rubbish. My gun wasn't even fired that day. Monroe has just proved it. You don't have any evidence."

"I think you'll find I do," Penny said. And was gratified to see the look of uncertainty flicker briefly across Sammy Reynolds' face.

"Go on, Penny," John said.

"Samuel Reynolds wanted money from his brother. He'd had some of his own, but that was a long time ago and he'd squandered it away. Now he was left with nothing, relying heavily on his brother to give him the handouts he needed just to get by." Penny addressed Sam directly. "I can only imagine how much it rankled to go cap in hand to your younger, far more successful brother for money."

Sammy Reynolds glowered and took a malevolent step forward. John stopped him. Penny took a deep breath and continued.

"However, having lost too much in the past on his brother's hare-brained schemes, Robert said no. The only way Samuel was ever going to get his brother's fortune was if he was dead. Whether or not he had another plan to get rid of Robert, I don't know, but when the smoke bomb was thrown onto the moor he suddenly saw the opportunity for it was. It was just too good to pass up. You saw the blast from Henri's gun, didn't you, Sam? That was the first shot I heard. Then you made your move. You fought Robert for his gun, and he must have seen the murderous look in your eye. Your intention was clear. It was then that he called out for help."

"That's what you said you'd heard," John said.

Penny nodded. "I didn't know who it was at the time, though. Samuel continued to fight Robert for the gun, and in the ensuing scuffle, a shot was accidentally fired into the air. That was the second shot. Then, when you'd finally wrenched the gun from his hands, he punched you. A right hook to the face that caught you on your cheek and left a nasty cut."

"That's a lie. I told I tripped getting back up here in all the smoke."

"That cut wasn't made just by your brother punching you though, was it? But by the ornate gold ring he was wearing at the time. That ring," Penny pointed at Sammy's hand. "Then when you'd finally got the gun, you fired. One single shot to the chest. That was the third shot. Now you had to think fast. You threw the gun as far as you could and took Robert's ring from his finger. Maybe you were going to put it on as though it was yours, but it was too small. You slipped it in your pocket instead. You thought you had a prime suspect, the protester seen fleeing the scene. You'd already seen her very briefly when her own substandard weapon had fired, but not clearly enough. Not enough to identify her, anyway. You referred to her as 'him' when I saw you in town. Besides, by then your mind was on covering up the murder you'd just committed. With your brother dead, she would make the perfect scape goat."

"How did you know about the ring, Penny?" John asked, not taking his eye of Sammy Reynolds.

"I know Claire the jeweller who enlarged it. She described it perfectly. It's a completely unique piece, apparently. Robert probably had it commissioned to his own design. You went for it to be enlarged and cleaned. Isn't that right, Mr Reynolds?" Sammy said nothing. "But unbeknown to you, Claire didn't have time to clean it properly before you came back for it. And that is where the forensic evidence will be that proves Robert punched you, and that you stole it from his hand after you'd shot him."

Monroe took a step forward, ready to take the ring and arrest the man, but before he could, Sammy darted away and snatched up the gun Max Damage had left on the table. He levelled it first at John Monroe, then swept it to point at Penny. Back and forth, covering them both. All the time he was taking steps backwards to the door.

Max Damage had put his glasses on, and once he could see what was happening, vaulted over the back of the sofa and hid.

"It's an interesting theory," Sammy Reynolds said. "But that's all it is. Now, I'll be leaving. If you don't want to get shot, I suggest you let me leave quietly."

He'd reached the door. Just as he was about to back through, Major Colton appeared flanked by two constables. Samuel had no chance. He wasn't aware they were there until it was too late. One deftly removed the gun while the other threw him against the wall, snapping on a pair of handcuffs in the blink of an eye.

"Well done, Major Colton. Perfect timing," John said.

"Formally arrest him for the murder of his brother Robert Reynolds, please, officer," John said. "Then take him away."

The second officer broke the barrel of Max's weapon and looked at Monroe. "It's loaded, sir." Penny gasped. The constable deftly removed the cartridges and handed them and the gun to his boss.

"Well done, constable," John said, with a slight quake in his voice.

"Does that mean the shoot's back on?" Max said, sauntering nonchalantly back out from his hiding place. His glasses were back in his pocket.

"Not for you, Mr Cavendish. You'll be charged with multiple firearms infringements. Carrying an uncovered firearm in public and being in possession of a loaded firearm outside a designated live firing area." Penny could see John was seething.

"We could have been shot just then, you idiot! I'll see to it that your firearms license is revoked today. No more grouse shooting for you." He handed back the gold gun. "You're lucky I haven't confiscated it. Although it's no use to you as a gun now. Perhaps you can use it as a doorstop?"

Max Damage grabbed the gun and stormed off angrily, cursing under his breath as he bumped into the table on his way out.

"You should have kept it," Penny said. "Auctioned it off for the police widows and orphans' fund."

John smiled. "That would have put it to better use."

Penny looked over at Henri, who was huddled on the bench. She looked far younger than her seventeen years. Tiny, forlorn, lost and utterly terrified. She looked back at John.

"Please be gentle with her. She's very fragile."

"Of course I will, Penny. I'm not a monster. But I will need to take her to the station."

"You can take us both. I'm not leaving her. I promised. And if you could arrange for a constable to return her van to the shop and break the news to her father, I'd appreciate it."

"Anything else, Monsieur Poirot?"

Penny smirked. "No, I think that's all, Hastings."

That night, both mentally and emotionally exhausted, Penny and John went to dinner at a local Italian restaurant in Winstoke. She'd sent a text to her mum explaining what had happened and Fischer was staying the night with her parents.

They'd all returned to the station directly from Thornehurst Grange, where Henri and Penny had waited for Henri's father to be collected and brought in. When he arrived, Mr Shattock was pale and badly shaken at the news of what his daughter had done.

But when he'd seen her, small, terrified and sobbing, he swept her in his arms and held her as though he'd never let her go again. He promised that whatever happened, he loved her and would support her in any way he could. No matter what she'd done, he would always be her father and he would always love her.

For Henri, this was everything she'd been hoping for and the dam finally broke. She'd been terrified of what he would think of her and was dreading the look of disappointment on his face. Penny had watched the reunion with tears in her eyes.

With her father now by her side, Penny had assumed she would no longer be needed, but during the official interviews and questioning, Henri had begged that Penny be allowed in as well as her father. John Monroe acquiesced, realising the girl needed Penny as a source of support.

The stark interview room had seemed vastly overcrowded. With John and another officer on one side of the table and Henri, her father, and the duty solicitor on the other. Penny was unobtrusively sat behind Henri. She wasn't needed and didn't speak. It was enough for Henri to know she was there.

The questioning went on for a long time, but eventually they had finished and, after a distraught farewell with her father, Henri was returned to the cell. It was then Penny's turn to give her official statement.

It was nearly eight pm when she and John left the station to walk hand-in-hand to the restaurant. The questioning of

Samuel Reynolds was being dealt with by a DI from another station. John would join him tomorrow. In the meantime, he was exactly where he should be, stewing in a cell.

"What do you think will happen to Henri, John?" Penny asked before taking another bite of her vegetarian pizza.

"I honestly don't know. These are serious charges, but she's still a minor in the eyes of the law and this is her first offence. The fact she didn't do what she set out to, that she changed her mind in fact, and came forward will count in her favour, but it's not up to me, as you know, Penny. It's up to the courts. I'll naturally do my best to put a good word in and expedite matters. The loss of the family business, the fact her father works all hours to keep a roof over their heads as a result, and the death of her mother will all be taken into account. Let us hope we get a sympathetic judge."

THIRTEEN

It was Saturday, a week later, and Penny was just carrying the last box of books from the Mobile Library to store temporarily in the house.

Thanks to Martin, the van was now running as good as new and Penny was thrilled. He'd had to replace several parts and the amount of work needed was actually more than he'd originally thought, but, although the bill was much more than Penny had expected, she knew he'd not charged her for his labour.

It was, therefore, with some surprise that he suddenly appeared waving an envelope.

"Good morning, Martin. Is everything all right?"

"I have some good news," he said, passing the envelope to her.

She peered inside and found the cash equivalent of what she'd paid him to mend the van.

"I don't understand?"

"Well, you know that chap who died at the grange left some money for the community?"

"Yes. Quite a lot, by all accounts. I think there's a visitor's centre and cafe planned for the castle and I know the library got a bit."

"The library got quite a lot, Penny. The council have been working it all out and as I service most of their cars, I got to hear how much it actually was. Believe me, they could afford a fleet of book vans if they wanted. So I put you and your mobile library forward to receive a grant for these repairs and any further ones you may need in the future. They agreed completely, and one of the council clerks dropped the money off just now."

"Oh, Martin, that's incredible news. Thank you so much. I hope they paid for your time as well? I know you undercharged me."

"They did. And for any other work that needs doing, just save your receipts and put them in. You'll be reimbursed in full."

"I don't know what to say, Martin. How can I ever thank you?"

"There's no need. Just knowing my Gran and her friends still have their library for many more years to come is all the thanks I need. So, you're starting on the inside, I see?"

"Yes. I'm looking forward to it."

"It's a big job. Are you doing it all yourself?"

"Oh, no. I've got some help. I'm just the gofer. And here she is. Martin, meet Henri Shattock."

"Pleasure to meet you, Henri. Okay, well, I'll let you get on. You know where I am if you need me."

"Thanks again, Martin. Bye for now," Penny said, then turned to Henri.

She'd cut her hair and now, instead of dreadlocks woven with coloured thread, she sported a sleek, shiny bob. She was wearing a short-sleeved black-and-white striped tee shirt under black denim dungarees. She still wore her favourite boots, though.

"Hi, Henri. How are you doing?"

"Pretty good, actually. Thank you again for helping me. Oh, I need you to sign this." She handed Penny an official form. "My probation officer said you'll need to sign every day to prove I've been here working for my community service."

Penny scribbled her signature, dated it, and handed it back.

"Good morning." Penny turned and found John approaching. He was casually dressed in jeans and an open necked, collarless white shirt.

"Hi, John."

"Hello, Inspector," Henri said shyly.

"It's the weekend, Henri, and I'm off duty, so John will do. You're just about to start, I see?"

"Yes." She looked at Penny. "You might want to disappear for this bit. I'm going to rip out all the old shelves and it won't be pretty."

Penny laughed. "You're right. I'll go and put the kettle on for tea. Do you have time for one, John?"

"Absolutely. Why do you think I'm here?"

Inside, Penny pottered around while John played with Fischer.

"Do you have any updates?" she asked.

"You know about Robert Reynolds' will?"

"Less than I thought. Martin's just given me back every penny I paid him for fixing the van. Apparently, there was quite a lot of money left to the library. I know the castle is get-ting some help as well, but that's it."

"Well, Sammy is pleading guilty. He'll not see the light of day ever again."

"I can't say I'm sorry, John. He was quite happy to let Henri take the blame for something he'd done. That's unforgivable."

"I understand. But the saddest part is that he was never going to inherit his brother's money. It was all for nothing."

"He wasn't going to get anything?"

"Just a small regular monthly sum to keep him going, but that's all. No more than he was getting when Robert was alive."

"So who did Robert leave it all to?"

"The majority to his business partner, a good bonus to each of his staff and the rest to be split between various chari-ties and community initiatives locally. And would you believe he left some to Mr Shattock? It was his initial investment on the deal that went wrong years ago, plus the equivalent of what would have been the accrued interest over the years. It makes for quite a tidy sum all told. I don't think Robert Reynolds was quite the scoundrel he was made out to be. He certainly had a conscience which is more than can be said for his brother."

"Golly, I didn't see that coming. I'm so pleased for Henri and her dad. So what about Max Damage's music?"

"That was never part of the deal. I don't know where Max got the idea, but he still owns all his music. The London business is part of Reynolds' company, but I believe there's dialogue between the new owner and Max. So I expect that will all be sorted out soon enough."

"I suppose it's all worked out as well as it could have done then. The best part is Henri. I can't tell you how happy it makes me that she's been given another chance. Thank you for going to bat for her, John. I know a lot of what transpired was down to you."

John shrugged. "The least I could do. She didn't belong in any sort of jail, Penny. She's got her whole life ahead of her. I think she's learned her lesson."

An hour later, they went to see how Henri was getting on and were amazed to see what she'd achieved. A couple of shelves were already in situ and fitted beautifully. In fact, they were a better fit than the old ones.

"Good grief, I didn't realise how talented you were, Henri," John said. "This is beautiful craftsmanship. Just out of interest, have you got any more work lined up after this?"

Henri shook her head. "Not at the moment. I'll help dad obviously, but nothing else."

"Well, it just so happens I have very recently bought the old police house just up the road there, and I'm in dire need of some help to get the inside fitted out. My DIY skills are a bit rudimentary, but with my job, I'm not going to have time to do much. Would you be interested?"

The grin that broke out on the girl's face said it all.

Penny smiled. She couldn't think of a better ending to a very fraught couple of weeks.

Did you enjoy Driven to Death? It would be great if you could leave a review on the site where you bought it. It really helps other readers to find the books. Thank you.

*

FREE BOOK – The Yellow Cottage Mystery, the prequel short story to J. New's British historical mystery series, is yours as a thank you for joining her Reader's Group newsletter. You can find more information on the website: www.jnewwrites.com

*

Have you met Ella Bridges yet? England in the 1930s. **The Yellow Cottage Vintage Mysteries**. Immerse yourself in country house murders, dastardly deeds at English church fetes, daring escapades in the French Riviera and the secret tunnels under London, in the award-winning series readers call, 'Miss Marple' meets 'The Ghost Whisperer.'

THE BOOKS:
- An Accidental Murder
- The Curse of Arundel Hall
- A Clerical Error
- The Riviera Affair
- A Double Life

Available in book shops internationally in print, e-book and audio formats. Check the website for more information. www.jnewwrites.com

*

Meet Lilly Tweed – Former Agony Aunt, Purveyor of Fine Teas, Accidental Sleuth.

If you like twists and turns, red herrings galore and big crimes in small British towns, then you'll love the **Tea & Sympathy Mystery** series. Full of lively personalities, intelligent characters and excellent tea!

THE BOOKS:
- Tea & Sympathy
- A Deadly Solution
- Tiffin & Tragedy
- A Bitter Bouquet
- A Frosty Combination
- Steeped in Murder
- Storm in a Teacup
- High Tea Low Opinions
- Green with Envy

Available in book shops internationally in print and e-book formats. Check the website for more information. www.jnewwrites.com

About the Author

J. New is the author of **The Yellow Cottage Vintage Mysteries**, traditional English whodunits with a twist, set in the 1930s. Known for their clever humor as well as the interesting slant on the traditional whodunit.

She also writes the **Finch & Fischer** and the **Tea & Sympathy** mysteries, both contemporary cozy crime series.

Jacquie was born in West Yorkshire, England. She studied art and design and after qualifying began work as an interior designer, moving onto fine art restoration and animal portraiture before making the decision to pursue her lifelong ambition to write. She now writes full time and lives with her partner of twenty-four years, along with an assortment of stray cats and dogs they have rescued.

Printed in Great Britain
by Amazon